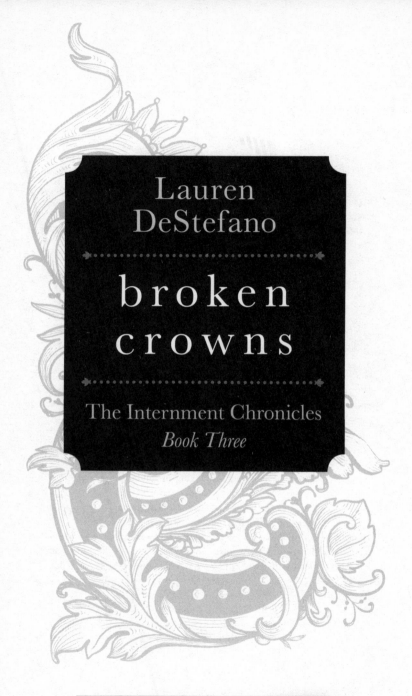

Lauren
DeStefano

broken
crowns

The Internment Chronicles
Book Three

SIMON & SCHUSTER BFYR

New York | London | Toronto | Sydney | New Delhi

SIMON & SCHUSTER BFYR

An imprint of Simon & Schuster Children's Publishing Division
1230 Avenue of the Americas, New York, New York 10020

For information about special discounts for bulk purchases,
please contact Simon & Schuster Special Sales at 1-866-506-1949
or business@simonandschuster.com.
The Simon & Schuster Speakers Bureau can bring authors to your live event.
For more information or to book an event, contact the Simon & Schuster
Speakers Bureau at 1-866-248-3049 or visit our website at www.simonspeakers.com.
Book design by Lizzy Bromley
The text for this book is set in Stempel Garamond.
Manufactured in the United States of America
2 4 6 8 10 9 7 5 3 1
Library of Congress Cataloging-in-Publication Data
DeStefano, Lauren.
Broken Crowns / Lauren DeStefano.
pages cm. — (The Internment Chronicles ; Book three)
Summary: With their floating city utopia threatened by the war on the
ground and the greed of two kings, Morgan and the others from Internment
must find a way to save the city from falling out of the sky or being
obliterated altogether.
ISBN 978-1-4424-9637-8 (hardcover)
ISBN 978-1-4424-9644-6 (eBook)
[1. Science fiction. 2. Utopias—Fiction.] I. Title.
PZ7.D47Br 2016
[Fic]—dc23
2014046571

acknowledgments

Thank you, always, to my parents and my family for always being my first supporters and fans. And for enduring the poems I wrote in high school. Thank you to my little cousins, especially, who are growing into such brilliant young readers and who are forever asking me to tell my stories to them whenever there's a lull in the day.

Thank you to my agent, Barbara Poelle, whose faith in me has somehow yet to falter even after all these years; you are the reason people think I'm a well-oiled writing machine when I'm actually the source of the weeping in the bathroom stall. Thank you also to Rachel Ekstrom, for her help and editorial insights when I needed it most, and for spending so much time helping me sort things out; thank you to the entire team of Irene Goodman, for the overwhelming support, not just for this story, but for the entirety of my career—not just at the beginning, but before even then. And thank you to my editor, Jaime Levine, without whom, believe me, this book wouldn't be happening right now; thank you for the infinite patience, the vegan dinner and subsequent frozen yogurt, and the countless conversations that reignited the flame for this story every time I thought it was dimming down for good.

Thank you to Harry Lam, professional know-it-all

and genius extraordinaire, for always questioning my ideas and encouraging me to see them through; you are the great constant of my life, and I am thankful beyond words. Thank you to my work wives and confidants, Beth Revis and Aprilynne Pike; you are the humor in the hollow void and all the sappy gushy things I quit writing down when I kicked my poetry phase. So all I'll say is thank you again. Thank you to Laura Bickle and Aimée Carter, for the copious support, and Tahereh Mafi, whose brilliance inspires me to be better. Thank you to Leigh Bardugo, whose books were my self-set reward for meeting my daily writing goals. Thank you to Alexandra Cooper and Amy Rosenbaum, who believed in this story at its beginning.

Thank you to my publisher, Simon & Schuster BFYR, for taking a chance on an unknown writer all the way back at the start, and for teaching me so many valuable lessons about the industry that I will carry with me for the rest of my life.

Thank you, always always always, to my readers, for their loyalty and warmth and laughter that I carry like a lantern in the darkest hours of writing.

We shall not cease from exploration

And the end of all our exploring

Will be to arrive where we started

And know the place for the first time.

—*T. S. Eliot*

1

"The city is falling out of the sky," Professor Leander said. They were his last words. The medicine of the ground was not enough to cure an old man of the sun disease. He refused most of the efforts anyway. He told me that he'd already accomplished what no one else had been able to do. He'd gotten us to the ground. He was quite curious, he said, to know if his spirit would be taken to the tributary, or if he'd go to whatever afterlife the ground believed in, or if there was nothing at all.

Amy was with him when he died, and she called it a peaceful death. A fitting death.

Down a labyrinthine set of hallways in the same hospital, Gertrude Piper opened her eyes after a month of sleep. It was as though the two gods had made an even trade—the life of a man from the sky in exchange for the life of a girl on the ground.

Before that, we all thought that Birdie Piper would die. After I landed in Havalais at the dawn of winter, she was the most vibrant thing in her strange world. She offered her friendship to Pen and me without question; she snuck us through our bedroom window and showed us the wonders of Havalais. The mermaids in the sea. The glittering lights cast upon the water at night. The spinning metal rides in her family's amusement park.

And then the cold war between Havalais and its neighboring kingdom of Dastor advanced on us all at once, in the middle of the spring festival. I watched as an explosion swallowed Birdie. I saw her body, broken and bleeding and burnt, being kept alive by some coppery machine. Even worse than my brother had been when he'd come too close to the edge.

But nothing is certain, not even death when it's hovering over a girl. Not in my world, and not in this one. Birdie came back slowly. It took a month for her to open her eyes, and even longer for her to speak, serene in her delirium.

She told us about a spirit that would come into her room late at night to sing to her and to tend to the flowers on the table by the window.

When she had faded back to sleep, Nim slouched forward in his chair and rubbed his temples, anguished. "It wasn't a spirit," he told us. "Our mother's been here."

Mrs. Piper disappeared some years earlier to see the world. The same madness that brings so many to the edge of Internment haunts the people on the ground as well. One place is not ever enough for anyone, it seems.

It's August now, and Birdie no longer talks about her spirit. Instead she has returned to solid ground along with the rest of us. She asks her brother about the war. She wants to visit the grave of her other brother, Riles. She is getting well and she is ready to face the grimness that often comes with being awake. She doesn't wallow in her despair, and does not mind that her soft face has been forever scarred.

Pen is different. She doesn't seem ready to face anything these days. It has been months since King Ingram left for Internment, taking Princess Celeste with him, and in that time, Pen has been prone to more and more moments of distance. Jack Piper's guards surround the premises, and we are scarcely permitted to leave unescorted. Not until King Ingram returns with his instructions for us. But every week, Pen gives Nimble a new list of books she'd like from the library. Physics. Calculus. Philosophy. She is drowning in pages and pages of things she never shares with any of us. And that's when she isn't off someplace where none of us can find her, even within the confines.

The sun is starting to set, and after nearly an hour of searching, I find her at the amusement park. It would normally be thriving in August, the Pipers have told us, if not for the king's absence and the war. Now it's locked. But Pen and I sneak in sometimes.

"Pen?" I step onto one of the metal bars, preparing to climb over the locked fence.

She's standing high up on the platform with the telescopes that face Internment, and she turns to me.

"What are you doing?" I say.

3

She shrugs. She presses a piece of paper against the telescope and writes something down, then tucks the paper into her dress. "Nothing. Don't climb up. I was just leaving."

She descends the staircase, the steps reverberating under her stacked leather heels that make her taller than me. A girl our age would never be permitted to wear such things back home.

She comes to the fence and grips the bars and leans close, so that her forehead is almost touching mine.

"What are you doing all the way out here?" she says.

"Looking for you. You didn't come in for dinner."

"Who can eat?" she says, and hands me her shoes and hoists herself up over the fence. "The food in this place is nauseating. A different animal a night. I'd rather chew on grass." She lands on her feet with a thud, and goes about straightening her skirt. She takes the shoes but doesn't bother putting them back on.

I hate myself for trying to smell the tonic on her breath, but it must be done. She finds ways to steal gulps of it. We've fallen into an unspoken understanding that I will dispose of anything she tries to hide, and it will never be mentioned.

But if she's had anything to drink, I can't tell. Her eyes seem bright and alert when she looks at me. "Has Thomas been trying to find me?"

"Isn't he always?" I say.

She tugs my hand. "I don't want to go back inside just yet. Let's go to the water. Maybe there are mermaids."

Birdie told us that the mermaids never come close to the

shore. They prefer to stay where the water is deep, where they cannot easily be captured or get their hair ensnared on a fishing line. But I don't mind pretending we'll spot one. I try to keep pace with her as she runs.

With my other hand I hold my hat to my head. But eventually I let it go, and it escapes. When I'm with Pen, it seems I must always leave some small thing behind.

We are in a valley of green, with shy bright flowers poking their way through. In the wind I see dotted lines. I see red lines and blue lines. I see the maps that my best friend is always drawing as she moves, as she thinks.

"Maybe if we hold our arms out, the wind will carry us up," she says, and I think she believes it to be true.

Eventually we stop to catch our breaths somewhere along the ocean's shore. Pen rests her elbow on my shoulder and laughs at my wheezing. I have never been a match for her.

The wind is so loud that I can scarcely hear her laughter.

She drops onto the grass and pulls me down after her. Once I've caught my breath, she leans back on her elbows and looks at me. "What is it?" she says. "What's that worried look for?"

"I don't like all this wind," I say, over a roar of it. "It doesn't feel right." This time of year is so mellow on Internment. It is surely beautiful back home, the pathways all traced with bright flowers.

"A lot of the breeze comes from the sea," Pen says. "That's all."

"I know."

"Morgan, we aren't on Internment. Things are bound to be different. We've been here for months. We survived all that snow; this is just a little wind."

"I know." What I don't say is that I'm afraid she'll be swallowed whole by this whirling sky. This world already tried to kill her once, and Pen is fearless and foolish enough to let it try again.

A flock of birds flies high above us, in a uniform formation. Pen stretches her arms straight up over her head, her fingers arranged like a frame. I rest my head next to hers and try to see through that frame from her perspective.

After the birds have gone, she says, "Suppose Internment were to fall out of the sky."

"What?" I say.

"Suppose it couldn't stay afloat any longer and it came down all at once, hard and fast. I think it would coast at an angle, rather than straight down. I've been looking at the way the birds come down from the sky, and it's sort of a sixty degree angle most times."

"I don't give it any thought," I say.

She turns her head in the grass to look at me. "You've never thought about Internment falling from the sky before?"

"I have, I suppose." I stare up at the graying sky, where shades of pink and gold still cling to the sparse clouds. "But more as a nightmare, not something that will happen. I don't weigh the probability or try to picture what it would look like."

Pen stares up at the sky again.

"I think it would fall on King Ingram's castle," she says. "I think it would kill him and all his men. But the impact would destroy Internment, too. The foundations for all the buildings would shift. They'd likely collapse."

"Internment won't fall out of the sky," I say. I am gentle with her, but firm. I have heard Amy wonder about Internment coming down. I wondered myself, as a child. But Pen is different. She gets ideas like these in her head and they become real to her. She forgets what's in front of her and sees only what's in her mind, and just like that she's lost.

A mechanical growling from somewhere high above us disturbs the tranquil gray sky, and I flinch. Not even the largest beast on Internment could make a sound like that. The sound comes from the king's jet, descending from Internment for its monthly fuel delivery.

At the start of each month, the king's jet returns to Havalais to deliver more phosane that it has mined from Internment's soil. A refinery was built in Havalais to process that soil into fuel. In the mornings when I step outside, I can see the plumes of black smoke billowing out into the air, and sometimes I can smell it, too—like compost and metal.

But in six months, King Ingram has yet to return with his men, and after the delivery is made, the jet flies back to Internment for more. It's a wonder there is any city left up there at all.

The warring kingdom of Dastor has seen the jet's comings and goings. Nimble tells us that the war has moved to the home front. Boys even younger than he is are being recruited to fight. If Dastor means to have Internment and its fuel source, it will have to take ownership of Havalais itself.

"It won't happen," he's told us. "Havalais is bigger, more advanced."

I'm not so certain. I see nothing of the war from the confines of this sheltered world where Jack Piper raised his children, but sometimes when the air is still, I think I hear gunfire.

Pen puts her hand over mine, and I realize that I've been holding my breath. I know she's trying to keep me calm. She has heard me tossing and turning in my bed at night as I worry what news this king will bring when he returns from Internment. Only, I don't feel worry now. I don't feel anything, not even the dread that King Ingram usually ignites in me.

"We should go back and tell the others," I say.

Pen gnaws her lip, and even as she sits up, her face is still angled skyward. "It's probably just another delivery," she says, and she is likely right. Five times before this, the jet has returned, and five times we have all waited in silence for word of the king's arrival, and it never comes.

I pull Pen to her feet, and we make our way back to the hotel, both of us looking over our shoulders as the jet moves at an angle. Like a bird. Like a city falling from the sky.

Basil and Thomas arrive at the front steps moments before Pen and I do. Back on Internment, Pen's and my friendship was the only bond between them, but since coming here they've forged something like an independent friendship of their own, perhaps because if nothing else they have home in common.

They wouldn't have been able to go very far. Jack Piper has forbidden us to leave the grounds, for our own protection, all on the king's orders that we are to be kept away from anyone who may have sinister intentions for us now that it's revealed that we come from the magical floating island above this world. Though, the people of Havalais have more cause to distrust their king than to harm us.

Truth be told, I don't mind the restriction half the time. It makes me feel safe. Reminds me of the train tracks that surrounded me back home.

Other times, my wanderer's spirit comes out for a visit and I wonder at when this will all be over.

"We were walking back from the theme park when we saw the jet," Thomas says. "Did you see it?"

"Yes," I say.

Princess Celeste became a pawn when King Ingram needed access to Internment. King Furlow up in his sky has only two weaknesses, and those weaknesses are his children. He would allow King Ingram to have anything he asked for in exchange for Celeste's safe return.

I have worried for her in silence. Pen would be angry if I so much as brought her name up. But I do hope that she's well, and that her decision making abilities have improved.

Basil's standing close. His eyes are on me, and whether or not he knows it, he still sets my stomach fluttering.

Another gust of wind comes, and even the fearless Pen hugs her arms across her stomach and shivers.

Thomas frowns at her. "I've been looking all over for you."

"Not all over, clearly, or you'd have found me," she says.

He stands at a pace's distance from her, and I can see the worry in his eyes. I can see that he is trying to get a whiff of tonic on her breath. When he can't find one, he looks to me, and while Pen isn't watching I give a slight shake of my head. She's sober.

The jet has quit rumbling in the sky; presumably it has landed.

"Come on," I say to Pen, and hold the door open. "Let's see if we can find something in the kitchen you're willing to eat."

She follows me into the house, past the smallest Piper children, who are playing a war game in the living room. Annie is a soldier whose legs were blown off in an explosion, and Marjorie is a nurse applying a tourniquet. I have seen them play this game a dozen times, and it is anyone's guess whether Annie will survive her wounds. Last time, an explosion hit their pretend medical tent and all the nurses and soldiers were killed.

I hate this game, but I think it makes them feel closer to Riles.

Up at the top of the stairs, Amy watches them from between the bars of the railing, not quite ready for human interaction. She has been quiet since her grandfather's death, and she's added another cloth around her wrist beside the one meant to symbolize her sister.

"Let's say I lost my arm too," Annie says.

"Which one?" Marjorie asks.

"The left."

"Would you girls like to help me in the garden?" Alice calls down from the top of the stairs. She cannot bear this game of theirs.

Annie sits up from her deathbed on the hearth. "Why do you tend to the garden? We have a gardener."

"It just makes me happy, I suppose," Alice says. She reaches the bottom step and holds her hands out to them, and they forget their game and happily follow her outside.

In the kitchen, Pen and I sit at the small table reserved for the maids, and Pen bites into a raw carrot from the cold box.

"I wish you'd stop looking so worried," she says.

"I can't play it as cool as you, I suppose."

She stares at me for a long moment, and then she says, "You're not the only one who has nightmares about what's happening back home. Just because I don't talk about it doesn't mean I don't care."

"I know that you care. That's what's so frustrating," I say. "We've hardly spoken in months."

"What are you going on about 'we've hardly spoken'? We share a room. We speak every day. We're speaking right now."

"You know what I mean."

She takes another bite of the carrot, with a crunch I swear is meant to be pointed. "You'll forgive me if I don't entirely trust you with my secrets these days."

I know just what she means. It has been a source of

contention that's never fully gone away these past several months. She discovered that Internment's soil contains the very fuel source King Ingram wants for his kingdom, and she confided this secret to me. But after she nearly drowned, I told the princess everything, hoping an alliance could be forged between Internment and Havalais, giving us all a chance to return home.

Instead, King Ingram used the princess as a hostage and has been depleting Internment of its soil as he pleases.

I don't know the enormity of what's already happened and what's to come, but even so I wouldn't take back what I did. I'm still holding out hope that I'll be able to return Pen home to her family, to the city that she loves so much that she's been going to pieces without it.

So I say nothing, and Pen can see that she's wounded me. "Nim says Birdie has had her last surgery, and can come home soon," she says to change the subject. "She'll still be confined to her wheelchair, but I doubt that will last for long."

I push my chair away from the table. "I'm going to make some tea for Lex."

"Oh, Morgan, don't be cross. I didn't mean it. I'm just on edge because of that bloody jet."

"I know," I say softly.

I hope that this time the king has returned, and the princess as well, alive and safe. Whatever news they bring will surely be better than all this wondering and fear.

I don't know what sort of mood Lex will be in when I reach the top of the stairs, but he's been especially sour lately. He's running low on paper for his transcriber, and soon he will no longer be able to spend his days hiding in his fictional worlds.

I knock when I reach his door.

"Alice?" he says.

"No, it's me." Back home he always knew when I was the one approaching him, but something about this house and its noises disorients him. "I've brought some tea."

"Oh," he says, rather unenthusiastically. "Come in."

He's sitting in a wing chair near the open window, and the worry on his face mirrors my own from earlier. He doesn't care for the wind; perhaps it reminds him too much of the edge. "The weather down here takes some getting used to," I say. I press the teacup into his hand, not letting go until I'm sure he's got a grip on it.

"I have a bad feeling," he says.

"Me too."

I hesitate, standing before him, debating with myself whether to tell him what I saw in the sky.

But in the end I'm not given a choice. Even without his sight, Lex is clever at sensing when anything is wrong. "What is it, Little Sister? What's happened?"

I wring my skirt in my hands. "We saw the jet about an hour ago. Pen, Basil, Thomas, and I. We've been waiting for someone to come home and tell us what it means."

Lex is silent for a long moment. "I heard." He takes a sip of his tea and then with minimal fumbling he sets it on the window ledge. "So it begins," he says.

"There's no need to be so theatrical," I say. "It may be good news."

"A greedy king in a wasteland of wealth holds a princess hostage so that he may invade a tiny floating city, and you still think he may return with good news. My sister the optimist."

I am tired of being called an optimist as though it were a bad thing. Pen has used this word against me as well. "I'm merely trying not to panic, Lex." I hold myself back from saying anything too combative. I don't want to fight, and it has taken me so long to stop hating my brother for lying to me about our father being dead. I would like for us to be reasonable with each other.

"Where is Alice?" he asks. Maybe he wants to avoid an argument too.

"She's in the garden."

"And she knows about the jet?"

"I told her when we came back inside. We're all waiting now. Drink your tea, all right? Alice will be up to check on you in a bit."

As I cross the threshold, he says, "Morgan?"

I turn.

"Be careful."

"I'm only going downstairs."

"I never know what mad and wild adventures you'll get off to on a whim."

I can't help but smile at the thought. Mad and wild adventures. It's not something he ever would have accused me of back home, when I was tucked safely in our little floating world.

2

They never exhale, the trees. It was the same on Internment; on a very windy day, the trees rustle and inhale, and then the leaves and the branches all tremble as though something were trying to strangle the life from them. The dark sky watches on, filled with anticipation, wondering if this will be a great night, or a horrible night, or the last night of the world.

"Morgan." Basil's voice pulls me out of my trance. He joins me at the window, and when his arm brushes mine, my skin swells with tiny bumps. "You've been standing here for an hour."

My body releases some of its tension and I lean my head toward his. "I have a bad feeling. Lex does too. Like something big is about to happen."

"Suppose something is about to happen," he says. "Then what?"

I shake my head. "I'm tired of being driven mad by the 'what if' game. I just want to know. I want King Ingram to come back and tell us what's happening. Good or bad. So all the wondering can stop."

Basil is quiet for a few seconds, and then with some difficulty he says, "I've been playing that same game, wondering about my parents and Leland."

I look at him.

"I think they must be okay," he says, and nods straight ahead at the sky, where our floating city is hiding somewhere in that darkness beyond our sullen reflections. "They would follow the king's orders. They've always been smart about that."

"Which king's orders?" I say.

"Whichever king is in charge these days," he says.

"Maybe King Ingram and King Furlow really are forming some sort of alliance," I say. "Maybe there will be good news."

He glances sidelong at me, and a smile comes to his lips. "I've always loved your optimistic side."

"You're the only one. Everyone else seems to think I'm foolish for harboring it."

He puts his arm around my back, and the last of the tension in me dies. I rest my temple against his shoulder. "I'm tired, Basil. And so worried that the decisions I've made were the wrong ones."

"The wrong decisions have been made by these kings," he says. "And for what it's worth, I would have done the same thing you did. If I'd known about the phosane, I would have told."

"Really?"

"If what's happening to Pen had been happening to you, if I'd thought this world were killing you, yes. I'd do anything it took to bring you back home."

"You've always understood me, Basil."

His arm tightens around me and I close my eyes. The anxiety feels so distant when he's around. Farther away and smaller in the sky than our long-lost floating city.

Then I hear the front door open, and my stomach drops.

The younger Pipers have long since gone to bed, and everyone else has been in the lobby for hours, waiting for word. All eyes are at the front door when Nimble steps inside, his shoulders dropped, his eyes weary. He is always the first to run to the tarmac when the jet returns, hoping for word about Celeste. And he is always heartsick when no word comes.

We all wait in silence. Nim raises his head and looks at each of us, settling on me. "King Ingram has returned. My father is with him now. I don't know what any of this means yet. I'm sorry."

He moves toward his bedroom, and by the heaviness of his steps I can suspect what the answer will be. But still I have to ask, "Was Celeste with him?"

He pauses, his back to me. "No," he says. "My father told me only that the king has brought a special visitor, but it isn't her." He takes a deep breath, and his voice is so tight, I think he may be fighting tears. "I doubt my father will be back tonight. You might as well all go to bed."

He can't get away from us fast enough.

Pen is standing by the couch, Thomas at her side. She's staring worriedly after Nimble, though, and she doesn't hear Thomas until the third or fourth time he's said her name. "Pen." She flinches, startled.

"We'll know more tomorrow, surely," Basil says.

The hotel falls into its nightly silence. I soak in the tub long after everyone else has gone to bed. The mornings in this place can be so noisy, with the Piper children running about, shrieking with laughter as they play their games, most of which involve explosions. And footsteps going this way and that, and voices, and silverware on plates.

But the nights are still. I can feel everyone's silence just as surely as I can hear their voices during the day.

Someone knocks at the door. "Morgan?" Pen's voice. "Are you all right? You've been in there forever."

"I thought you were in bed," I say.

"I couldn't sleep, and I wanted to make sure you hadn't drowned."

"I'll be out in a minute." The water's gone cold anyway. I wring out my wet hair, dry off, and slip into my nightgown.

When I open the door, Pen is waiting in the hallway, holding a lantern. Its orange glow picks up the bags under her eyes, and I can see all at once how troubled she's been, despite her best efforts to conceal it.

"I'm not tired," she whispers. "Are you?"

"No," I say, although it's a lie. I will stay awake all night if there's a chance she'll finally be honest with me. She is much more likely to reveal her secrets at night, when the sleeping world will be undisturbed by her whispering voice.

She smiles. "Do you want to go for a midnight walk?"

We don't bother with our shoes. We tiptoe barefoot down the steps and through the front door.

Unlike earlier, the night's wind is mellow and warm. The moon outshines our lantern, nearly full and bright white.

As soon as we've stepped into the grass, I can feel the cool earth under my feet, astoundingly like the ground back home. Pen moves forward, and when I don't follow, she turns to face me. "Aren't you coming?"

I wriggle my bare toes in the grass and stare down at it. I have never seen the heaps of soil being flown down from Internment. I've only heard about it from Nim. I imagine Internment filled with craters so wide that you could look through them and see the ground below.

"I was just thinking about home," I say. "About what King Ingram is going to tell us, if he plans to tell us anything at all."

Pen takes my hand, leads me away from the hotel. "Come on. There's something I want to show you."

She leads me to the amusement park, and I climb the fence after her without question, happy to see whatever it is she wants to show me. Maybe it will be something other than tonic this time. Maybe it will give me some insight into this distance she's built between herself and everyone else in this world.

I expect her to lead me to the telescopes. That's where I find her sometimes. But instead she leads me to the giant teacups, sitting inanimate in the moonlight. She is still clutching the lantern when she kneels beside one of the saucers—chipped but still bright green—and reaches beneath it, somewhere in the mechanism that would cause it to spin.

Eventually she finds what she was looking for: several pieces of paper folded together. Whatever is on those pages must be important, if she would keep them all the way out here.

Is this because I discovered her request paper all those months ago? Does she think I'll go rifling through her things when she's not in our room? I haven't. I would never. But sometimes, when I hear her tossing and turning, muttering through her nightmares about the harbor, I would do anything to know what is happening in her mind.

"Here." She hands me the lantern, and then she swings one leg over the teacup's rim, then the other. She takes the lantern back so I can climb in after her.

Inside the teacup is a metal wraparound bench, and she sits so close to me that my wet hair dampens her shoulder.

She spreads the papers open on the small table before us—the one that we would twist if we wanted the teacup to spin. "Now that the king is back, we have to find a way to stop him," she says. Her eyes are on the pages. "If we don't, I think we're in real trouble."

I stare at the pages, lit up by the moon and the lantern, and as always, I don't understand. I see Pen's steadily drawn lines. I see a circle and a small floating silhouette that could be Internment. I see numbers drifting around it like birds.

Pen shuffles through the pages like a madman. "I've been reading up on the sunsets. The sun goes down about a minute earlier every day, except about once a week or so when it goes down two minutes earlier."

She looks at me to be sure I'm following along. "Okay," I say. I've never paid too much attention to the sunset, but I know that we're at the time of year when we lose a bit of light each day. "So?"

"So," she says. "For the past few months, I've been keeping a grid of where Internment sits in the sky, and where the sun should be. Every day I look through the same telescope at the same angle."

She points to Internment's shape on each of the pages before us, as though I should know what we're looking at.

"I don't understand."

She looks at me, and I can see how tired her face is, how worried. But her eyes are bright, the way they always are when she's onto something important. "Internment is sink-ing. Not very much, but a bit each month. Enough that it's bound to be a problem if this keeps up."

I can only stare at the pages as these words sink in. In her ever steady hand Pen has drawn the outline of the clock tower, protruding above the mass of apartment buildings. Scraggly roots jut from the torn underbelly of the floating city. The sun, a perfect circle, is at a distance, held in the pure white sky by tiny equations I can't decipher.

There are two versions of Pen. There is the silly,

spontaneous, and brutally blunt girl I know, and then there is the side of her that can ingeniously solve these mysteries. It is frightening what she is capable of.

"Can you be sure?" I say.

"The professor helped me with the algorithm." She gnaws on her lower lip guiltily. "I'd been visiting him before he died."

I suppose she expects me to feel betrayed. And I do, in a way, but I am also relieved. I knew she was off somewhere; I'm only grateful it wasn't with a bottle.

"It must be all the mining," I say. "We don't know how much soil King Ingram's men bring back on each shipment."

"It would have to be a lot of soil to affect Internment's weight," Pen says. "More soil than could possibly be fitting into those jets. Internment is thousands of times their size. I don't think it's that."

"What, then?"

Pen shuffles through the papers until she finds a full-page drawing of Internment. The accuracy and scale is stunning, as though she'd sat in the sky and sketched its likeness. She has drawn a bubble around the city in rough overlapping lines.

"When your brother went to the edge, it was the wind that threw him back. The wind was moving sideways, like a current around the city. Have you ever noticed the way clouds that get too close to Internment seem to zip past us?"

"Those clouds get caught up in the wind that surrounds

the city," I say. "And you think that wind is part of what's keeping Internment afloat?"

"I have several theories about what keeps Internment afloat, but I do think the wind is a big factor," Pen says. "When we left the city in the metal bird, we went under the city, through the dirt. But King Ingram's jet lands and departs from the surface."

"It flies through the wind," I say, understanding.

She nods eagerly. "And disrupts it. Maybe even weakens it. It's a slight change for now, but over the course of years, it could knock Internment from the sky completely."

Her voice is excited, the way it always is when she is explaining things. But in the silence that follows, she remembers the magnitude of what she's said, and I feel it too. Internment is not only being ravaged by this world's greedy king; it could be knocked right out of the sky.

"King Ingram wouldn't care if he knew," I say.

"No. Why should he? He'll have what he wants. Even if Internment crashed right into Havalais, he'd stand clear and let people die like he did at the harbor."

I look at Pen. "How do we stop it?"

She shrugs. "I say we kill King Ingram."

"Be serious."

"I am, rather."

"Yes, okay," I say. "We'll just walk right up to his castle, and we'll knock on the door, and then we'll stab him with the knife you keep under your pillow. I can't find any fault in that. But suppose we come up with a backup plan."

"There's only one person I trust who has access to the

king," Pen says. "And I'd trust him with a secret, too. After all, he's lived his entire life never letting anyone know he's third in line to the throne."

"Nimble?" I say. One night after too much drinking, Birdie confided in us that her father was the king's secret bastard, and that she and her siblings were princes and princesses. Later when she was comatose after the bombings, Nim confirmed it.

"He hates King Ingram as much as I do," Pen says. "The king is the reason his brother is dead. The king is the reason the princess was taken away from him. He has no reason to care about Internment, but he cares about her, and she's up there. He'll want to help us."

A light breeze coasts along the ground, bringing the salt of the endless ocean, rustling the grass and causing some rusted metal thing within the park to squeak.

The papers rattle, and Pen organizes them with affection and folds them along their crease.

"Should we talk to him tomorrow?" I say.

"We won't have to wait until then." Pen nods up at the telescope at a distance. In the moonlight I can just see a dark outline clutching one of the telescopes aimed at Internment. "He comes here every night and drops coin after coin into that thing so he can stare up at the city. He would never be able to see her, though. At best those lenses make a blurry faraway view bigger and blurrier."

I feel a pain in my chest, watching him. He lives in this vast world that goes on forever until it wraps around to where it started again. There are trains and biplanes and ferries and elegors that can take him anywhere. But he cannot reach the girl he loves up in her kingdom in the sky.

"I hear him sneaking out sometimes at night," Pen says. "The poor fool." She heaves a deep breath then blows out the lantern.

We climb one after the other from the teacup, through the man-made labyrinth of gears and metal pieces until we reach the stairway to the telescopes.

It is here that we hesitate. As pressing as the matter is, neither of us wants to interrupt this intimate sadness.

But we don't have to. He heard us approach, and after a few seconds, when the telescope must have expired, he comes to the top of the staircase and looks down at us.

"Bit late for a stroll, isn't it, girls?" he says in his breezy Havalais accent.

Pen is clutching the papers to her chest. "We have something to tell you," she says.

We sit on the wooden planks beside the telescopes, Pen's drawings spread out between the three of us like a deck of morbid cards.

Throughout Pen's explanation, Nimble said nothing and asked no questions. He only stared with that pensive expression he gives when his father is discussing politics. Now he reaches forward to touch Internment's outline on one of the sketches. "So much detail," he says. "There must be an atlas in your head. It must be so exhausting."

He looks up at us, smiling grimly. "Celeste and I predicted something like this happening. Not exactly this, per se, but that King Ingram's greed about the phosane would make him reckless. We knew Internment was in jeopardy."

"We already have the riddle, then," I say. "What's the answer?"

"You girls aren't the only ones unhappy with King Ingram," Nim says. "It isn't just the people of Internment who have cause to hate him. There's been a lot of unrest down here since the bombing at the harbor. I have a boy who works as one of the king's guards who has been feeding me intelligence. His niece was killed in the bombing."

"That's awful," I say.

"What kind of intelligence?" Pen says.

"So far it's all just been a lot of angry chatter," Nim says. "The refinery has caused some people in the heart of the city to become sick. Water comes out of the pipes smelling like sulfur. After the bombings, this phosane was supposed to make everything better, and it has only caused more problems. King Ingram has the phosane, but he doesn't know what to do with it. He's a politician, not a scientist. The scientist who initially discovered its usefulness is dead now, and there's speculation that Dastor would know a thing or two about refining it, but as for our kingdom, Havalais has yet to see this miracle fuel in action and they're beginning to doubt it exists."

"It exists," Pen says. "Down here you call it phosane, but up on Internment we call it sunstone, and it's a powerful fuel source if it's refined properly." She sits up straight, stricken with a new thought. "What if the engineers on Internment are refusing to help them refine it? Or what if they're giving faulty instructions?" She looks between Nim and me, giddy and proud. "What if they're up there fighting?"

I struggle to suppress my smile. It's bad luck to hope for such a thing, but I could believe it. I do believe it. "If that's true," I say, "King Ingram needs Internment. He can't just take all he pleases and then dispose of its people. It took decades for our engineers to perfect the glasslands and harness our fuel. Your king may have all the riches to build and employ a refinery, and all the raw materials, but if he doesn't know how to use them, it's all for nothing."

"Clever little city," Nim says, looking up. He does not share in our joy, though. "If that's true, it's surely an ugly scene up there right now. Think torture. Think homes being burnt down. Your people can be as stubborn as you please, but no one down here can hear them scream from up there."

Pen shakes her head wildly. "It doesn't matter. Don't you see? Being tortured, deprived—it's the lesser evil. Our people would withstand anything to keep the city afloat."

"She's right," I say. "Down here, if you don't like where you live, you can pick up and leave. If you don't like the weather, or your children—you can just go. But on Internment, our home is all we have."

The people of Internment are resilient if we have to be. We don't value property or money the way they do down here; often our secrets are the only things of worth to us. I think of, but don't say aloud, the time the prince and princess held us hostage in their clock tower's dungeon. All they wanted was a way to the metal bird, and proof that it existed, but I would have died before I'd have let them have it.

"Your king underestimated Internment," I say. "But that's good. Isn't it? We can work with that. We can—I don't know."

I look at Pen, hoping she'll blurt out a solution. But she foolishly expects the solution to come from me. "Go on," she says.

"We can try to get sent to Internment, and then we'll know for sure what's happening up there. If they're not telling King Ingram how to refine the phosane, maybe there's a rebellion being organized."

"If that's true, there's plenty of intelligence here on the ground that would be of use to them," Nimble says. "There are men in King Ingram's court who are disgruntled enough to help. It's just a matter of finding who to trust, and I know those boys. You could leave that to me."

"How would we get ourselves sent back to Internment, though?" Pen says.

"We could go to King Ingram and pretend we'd like to help him," I say. "We can make him think that he can use us the way he used Celeste. As leverage or a sort of hostage. And he'll send us back home." I look at Nim. "Do you think he would do that?"

Pen laughs and grabs my face in her hands and kisses my temple. "Brilliant," she says.

"Really?"

"Really," Nim says. "That might work." The hope in

his eyes is too much to take. I don't tell him that if the people of Internment are as stubborn as we're hoping, King Ingram may have gotten desperate and gone for the jugular. And there are only two things on Internment that could be taken from King Furlow that are of any value: his children. Prince Azure, and Princess Celeste. They may already be dead.

3

Pen is not ready to divulge her findings to Thomas or the others, but she understands when I insist on telling Basil. If I'm going to attempt to return to Internment, he deserves to know.

In the morning I meet him in his room as everyone else is going to breakfast. I close the door behind me. We sit on his bed and I tell him everything in a hushed tone. Through it all, he doesn't say a word, listening patiently to my eager, harried rambling.

When I get to the end, it takes all my willpower not to look away from him when I say, "And Pen and I want to convince King Ingram to send us back. If we make him think we're on his side, and that we want to try to talk the engineers back home into helping him, we're hoping he'll go along with it."

He is the first to break our gaze. He looks down at my

hand as he covers it with his own and then he looks back at me. "When we were back home, your mind wandered toward the ground. But now that we're on the ground, your mind wanders back home. Sometimes I think what you want is to be away from wherever it is you're standing."

"Maybe there's some truth to that," I admit.

"I think about home, too." He speaks with great caution. "Not just my parents and Leland, but the life I had there. The sounds. The future I might have had." He shakes his head. "It was enough for me, staying there. I didn't mind it. But for as long as I can remember, there has been this current leading me away. You," he says.

"I tried, Basil. I tried to stay within the train tracks, to do what was expected of me."

"I know you did. I was there with you."

I stare down at our hands. "I didn't want to be the current pulling you away from all the things that you loved."

"Morgan," he says, in that practical way of his. "You were the thing I loved."

The words feel both wonderful and painful at the same time. "The truth is that I had to pull you along with me," I say. "I couldn't untangle myself from you if I tried. We've always just sort've gone together. It's as though someone mixed us up until we were a secondary color, and there's no way to tell which one of us started out which color."

I am terrible with words. My brother's the writer. I'm only clumsily trying to come up with words for things I'll never have the skill to say.

Basil laughs, but he isn't making fun of me. I know he understands.

"I am going to live my life worrying about you," he says. "But I do think you're right that there is unrest on Internment. It's a peaceful city. It has nothing to protect itself against a kingdom like Havalais, much less the ground itself. If nothing is done, and Pen's calculations are correct, Internment will crash-land on the ground before King Ingram ever has a way to refine his phosane."

"A lose-lose," I say.

"If you were to go back home, you would need something that would give Internment a fighting chance against King Ingram. Do you have anything like that?"

"Nim thinks he can get us some allies on the ground. A lot of King Ingram's men are disgruntled after the bombing. And on Internment we'll have an ally in Princess Celeste. If she's still alive."

"She'll be alive," Basil assures me. "If King Ingram wants something from Internment, he won't go killing King Furlow's children before he has it."

"I hope you're right."

"What if I go with you?" Basil says. "No matter what information or power you may be able to gather, the fact remains that both Havalais and Internment are patriarchies."

Pen would hate him for saying it, but I know that he's right. Kings are more reasonable with men than they are with girls. King Ingram is more likely to believe that Basil could influence the engineers.

"But is that what you want?" I say.

"I could never sit idly by while you disappear into the clouds, leaving me to wonder if you're alive each day," he says, and despite everything, I can't help but indulge in that beautiful thing he's just said to me. He goes on, "I also don't want Internment to come crashing down on our heads, killing us all and my family too."

"Nim is hoping to get an audience with the king this afternoon," I say. "Let's hope he can come through. Oh, and, Basil, about all this. Pen doesn't want Thomas to know about it."

He frowns. "It isn't our business to get involved, then. But I do wish she'd be more forthright about things. It would be healthier for her."

"You and me both," I say. "But for now I think it's best we keep this to ourselves until we know more."

"Agreed," he says.

Nim is gone after lunchtime, off to King Ingram's castle to play the good son to Jack Piper for once, in an attempt to stay in his graces.

Pen and Thomas are playing a board game. They're leaning toward each other on opposing sides of the coffee table, the crowns of their blond heads almost touching.

It's a beautiful day, and Alice has taken Amy and the youngest Pipers outside. Through an open window I can hear them laughing in the garden. This Havalais air has had a positive effect on Amy; she hasn't had one of her fits in months.

Basil is trying to engage me in a game of cards. The decks

they use on the ground are similar to our own, and with a bit of compromise we can duplicate most of the games we played back home. But I am having the hardest time sitting still. My leg shakes anxiously. My mind is spinning out dozens of scenarios about Nim's efforts at the castle.

Should I tell Judas and Amy any of this?

The thought of Judas brings a rush of heat to my cheeks. We've barely spoken in weeks, and I don't see him anywhere now, but somehow I feel his presence hiding nearby, as always, just out of frame. We have scarcely spoken since our kiss, save for a few benign polite exchanges—*good morning; yes, please; thank you*—but time has done nothing to extinguish my curiosity about him. Time has not assuaged my guilt, and the sight of him still confuses me. I do not know what it will take to rid myself of that kiss, but I would pay any price to undo it. I would pay any price to stop wanting another.

Basil lays his stack of cards on the table and then gently takes the cards from my hands too. I blink dumbly at him.

"Would a walk help take your mind off it?" he says.

I shake my head. "I don't want to be gone when Nim gets back."

"We won't go far," he says. "Come on. The air will do you some good."

He's right. As soon as we've stepped outside, I feel less anxious. There's some comfort in hearing the living things in the grass and in the sky. A blue bird shoots from one tree to the next, and I wish I could capture a perfect image of him to take back home. There are no birds on Internment, only speculation as to what they must be like.

Basil and I walk a lap around the hotel, past the charred altar where Nim burnt his beloved car in offering so that his sister might live. Whether or not it was an answered prayer, Birdie did pull through. It makes me wonder if their god is real. It makes me wonder if any god is real, or if it's only easier to believe in that than in the arbitrary series of events that make up all our lives.

"What do you think it's like back home?" I say, to break the silence.

Basil is not one to lie about the way of things. "Ugly. I wonder what King Furlow is doing to reassure everyone. If he's able to do anything at all."

"I never realized how small Internment was until we came here," I say. "From down here it just looks like a big clot of dirt in the sky. If I had lived down here all my life, I would never have suspected there was any life up there. I would think it a mistake of nature, something small enough to fit into my palm if only I could reach out and take it."

How strange that I've lived so much of my life on a clump of dirt in an infinite sky. After all these months, I can feel myself starting to forget how alive it was up there, how bright and cheerful.

We've stopped walking, and as I shield my eyes and stare up at Internment, I can feel Basil watching me. My heart is fluttering in my chest, anxious and frightened and strangely thrilled. It is an act of bravery for me to look at him when he makes me feel this way.

"I was wrong, all those times I said your eyes might be

the same color as the sea down here," he says.

"No?"

"No," he says. "They're still the brightest blue I've ever seen."

I look at the ground, flustered, smiling. Without looking at him, I can feel his victorious smirk.

"You're being too kind," I say.

"Ridiculous accusation. When have you ever known me to be kind?"

"It's true; you're a real beast most days. Flat-out tyrannical."

He laughs. Somehow my arm ends up around his back, and his around my shoulders, squeezing me close. The sun burns the crown of my hair, and despite the warmth, my blood is running chills up and down my spine.

I want to tell him everything. About Judas kissing me in the grass, and the way he still haunts my thoughts even though he is surely using me to quell his loneliness. I want to tell Basil that I'm sorry, that I've made a mess of everything, that I'm scared.

But here beside him, insects hopping around our feet, all the worlds have gone still. This planet has stopped rotating around its sun. Everything is calm. We're safe here. We'll be okay.

4

After dinner, I help Alice with the dishes. For security purposes, Jack Piper has dismissed most of the hotel's staff, and chores like these are supposed to fall to his children, but Alice always gets to them first. Years of being married to my brother have left her restless and with an endless desire to make things clean.

She hands me a clean white plate, and I go over it with the dishrag. "Do you want to go back home?" I say.

She shakes her head. "I couldn't leave your brother, and he's told me he won't return. Not after what the king did to your parents, and especially to you."

"I didn't ask you what Lex wants. I asked what you want."

She smiles. It is a kind, wistful smile. "Should there be any difference?"

"What a thing to say. Of course there's a difference."

She hands me another dish. "After your brother jumped,

one afternoon while he was still in the hospital, I came home to tend to the plants, and there was a letter waiting for me at the door, from my parents. I was welcome to return home if I estranged myself from Lex. But if not, they felt it best for me not to associate with them anymore."

I suspected as much. Alice's parents stopped coming around, and jumpers carry a stigma. With the exception of Pen and Basil, I lost virtually all my friends. Still, to hear it said out loud disgusts me. There is no one kinder than Alice, and no one who deserves kindness more.

"That's the thing about marriage, love. You hope you won't ever have to choose, but if there's a choice to be made, it's the one whose blood is in your ring. It doesn't matter how many worlds there are; our place is with each other."

"Lex doesn't deserve you," I say. "Truly."

She smiles. "But there is nothing left for me up there," she adds. "Since you asked. Everything I need is here."

I don't know that there's much left on Internment for me either. I tell myself that my father is still alive up there, and that I'll be reunited with him. But when that happens, will he want to leave Internment behind? He risked his life trying to do just that.

After Alice and I have finished with the dishes, I slip outside unnoticed, and I walk to the ocean's edge, where the boats bob along lengths of rope. This place is asleep, like all of Havalais, lying in wait for a solution to this war. I lie in the sand for what feels like hours, fixated on that dark shadow of earth in the sky.

Long after the sun has set, Nim still hasn't returned. The smallest Pipers are asleep.

I lie in bed while Pen reads one of Birdie's catalogs by candlelight. She's got a drawing pad resting on her knee, and she keeps returning to a sketch she started earlier this evening of Ehco, a divinity that lives in the sea and contains all the world's sadness. It's Birdie's favorite story from *The Text*, and I suppose the drawing will be a gift for Birdie when she returns home.

"Pen?"

I can hear the rapid strokes of the pencil on the page. "Mm? Sorry, am I keeping you awake?"

"No." I turn onto my side so I'm facing her. "It's just that you've been so guarded with your secrets lately. Why did you tell me your theory about Internment sinking?"

She goes on sketching. "It wasn't the right time before now. No sense making you panic until King Ingram was back and we could do something about it."

"It's just . . . After I told Celeste about the phosane, and she went to the king, I thought you hadn't forgiven me. I thought I'd been locked out of your head."

The pencil stills in her hand. She stares down at the page as she speaks, with difficulty. "I thought about everything," she says in a soft voice. "I thought about what it would have done to me to pull you out of the water, with you the one not breathing. I . . ." She draws a line on the page, feebly. "I saw it all very clearly, and I understood why you did it. I can't say I'd have done something different if the tables had been turned."

She clears her throat. "And besides, you could strike a match and set Internment on fire. You could lose your wits and destroy it all. I'd still be here. There's nothing in the worlds that I couldn't forgive you for."

The words are so sincere and candid that I'd like to get up and embrace her. But I don't move for fear of breaking this fragile moment between us. I have known Pen since before we were old enough to speak, and perhaps that is why so much of our friendship is built on what goes unsaid. But it feels so good to hear her say those words.

"I could never turn my back on you, either," I tell her.

"I know what I'm like, Morgan. I know it's not easy."

"So it's not easy," I say. "What is?"

She smiles briefly, and then allows herself to be distracted anew by her drawing.

I close my eyes, and eventually I feel myself fading into sleep, soothed by the sound of pencil on paper and catalog pages turning.

But it isn't a very sound sleep, because when there's a knock on the door, I'm startled awake.

"You girls awake?" Nim whispers through the door.

Pen is still sitting up by the candle. "Come in," she says.

I comb my fingers through my hair and wipe away the drool in the corner of my mouth, hastily trying to make myself presentable.

Nim opens the door and peeks his head in. "I didn't see the king. Or my father. I wasn't permitted into any of the meetings. My father isn't exactly happy with me these days."

"But you were gone all day," Pen says. "What were you doing?"

Nim smirks. "I was speaking with a few of the king's men. You remember how I said they were unhappy with things since the harbor? One of the men is assigned to guard King Ingram's special guest, come down from Internment. My contact is escorting the guest to a meeting spot for us, but we have to go right now."

"Him?" I say, trying to keep myself from hoping that the guest from home could possibly be my father. The disappointment would be unbearable if I were wrong.

"I think you'll love this," Nim says. "Hurry on and get dressed. I'll meet you outside."

I'm on my feet as soon as he's closed the door. I'm finished changing before Pen. "I have to get Basil," I say. "He'll want to come."

Pen sighs theatrically. "Must you?"

I stare at her flatly. "He's my betrothed."

"So?"

"You said you were fine with my telling him about all this. He's coming."

"Fine. But if you wake Thomas, I'll strangle you."

"Noted."

I turn the knob to the boys' room very slowly, wincing as I push the door away from the frame. I tread lightly past Judas's and Thomas's beds.

"Basil," I whisper, as quiet as breathing.

He murmurs something, tries to embrace me when I lean

in. It's my breathy laugh that wakes him. "Morgan?"

I put my finger to his lips, nod my head at the door in gesture.

He climbs out of bed and follows me out to the hallway. In whispers I tell him that Nim is taking us to see King Ingram's guest from Internment.

"'Hostage' may be more accurate," Basil whispers.

"Perhaps, yes." There are many people on Internment who secretly dream of life beyond the edge of the city, but most would be too terrified to ever leave. Especially now that King Ingram and his men have likely taken over the city.

We meet on the front steps, and Pen shivers excitedly. She has been carrying this information about Internment sinking in her head for months, and now finally she will be able to put her knowledge to use.

"Are you going to tell us who this mystery guest is?" she asks as we start walking.

"I don't think you'd believe me if I did," Nim says. "I'm not sure I'll believe it myself until I see him."

"How trustworthy are the men at the castle you've been speaking with?" Basil asks, the most practical of us all.

"Extremely. I've grown up in and out of the castle walls. I know which men are good and which are bad news."

"How can you tell which are good and which are bad?" Basil asks.

"The bad ones are friends of my father's."

Despite the grim sentiment, Nim is the most upbeat he's been in months. After the bombings and after Celeste's departure, he became despondent. I've been worried about him, but Pen's theory and the hope it brings has put light back into his eyes.

We can't fail. I run the words in my head over and over as we walk through the darkness and into the woods. We can't fail.

We walk for miles in fields and wooded areas off the main road. We must be near the city, because I can taste the burnt metallic quality to the air and I'm sure it's from one of the fuel refineries. Whatever King Ingram is doing with that phosane, it can't be right. I have never been inside the glasslands, but I have been near them, and there was never any smoke, never any horrid fumes.

Pen's father works in the glasslands. He's one of their top engineers. But Pen has not brought him up since our fight several months ago, when I found her request paper and she reluctantly confessed that he had hurt her in some way she wouldn't share with me. I have wondered in silence since then, hoping for and dreading her confidence in the matter. But Pen cannot be pushed. She cannot even be coaxed. I know this.

I walk between her and Basil, and for the next several paces it almost feels as though we're still back home, returning late from a play at the theater. We're just ordinary schoolchildren and our world is intact.

I have yet to see the outside of Havalais. Annette and Marjorie go into Birdie's room sometimes, and one afternoon they found a shoebox under her bed filled with all the post-cards their mother had sent from the farthest reaches of this world. Watercolor paintings of sprawling cities and barren deserts and long slender boats coasting over still waters. There is still so much to see, and confined as we are by King Ingram and his rules, I wonder at whether I'll ever have the chance.

Nimble leads us into the thick of some woods. We move guided only by the moonlight through the trees, and I can't help asking, "How do you know where we are?"

"Birds and I used to play here," he says. "The castle is less than a mile away. In the summer our father would send us outside so he could convene with the king. I know all the trees and roots by heart."

"Morgan and I used to have a spot in the woods," Pen says. "There was a cavern."

"It's still there," I say.

"Maybe."

"It is," I say. It is important to me that she believes this. That she believes there is still a safe place for us in our own world, hidden from all the warfare.

A whistle pierces the air. Something rustles in the brambles ahead of us, and Basil advances protectively at my side.

Nim is unconcerned. "This way," he says, and leads us toward the sound.

The trees are very tall here, blocking out most of the moonlight. But I can make out the dark silhouettes of two men standing side by side. I know it's unlikely. Unrealistic. But I hope that one of those men is my father. In this darkness they could be anyone.

"You're on time, but we won't have long," one of the men says. "The king is an insomniac since his return. He got up several times last night to wander the halls. No telling if he'll want to check in on our guest."

This guest, whoever he may be, doesn't say a word, leaving me to agonize.

"Is this him?" Nimble says.

"I'm standing right here," the other man says. "You could just ask me yourself."

My blood goes cold. Pen is in a dead silence beside me. I think she's stopped breathing. We know that voice, and it doesn't belong to my father.

Nimble reaches into his pocket for his matchbook, and then he strikes a match and brings the flame to a lantern the first man is carrying. And I see the face of King Ingram's guest. Prince Azure.

"May I present our honored guest," the man says, rather unenthusiastically, as though he must appease some imaginary court, "Prince Azure of the magical floating city."

"Internment," Prince Azure corrects. "There's nothing magical about it. We aren't a bedtime story."

"Prince Azure of Internment, then," the man corrects.

Nimble is frozen in place for a moment. Here in the lantern light, Azure bears a striking resemblance to his sister. He has the same clear, sparkling eyes, the rounded cheeks, the gold hair.

Nim snaps out of it after a few seconds and falls into a bow. "Your Highness," he says. "I'm—"

"Yes, I know who you are," the prince says with impatience. He grabs the lantern from the man beside him and holds it to Pen, Basil, and me.

He is wearing a pin-striped suit with a ruffled lace ascot that I recognize from his appearances back home. He stands tall and regal, nothing at all like the dying boy he was when I left him.

"I hope you're not expecting us to curtsy," Pen says.

"Pen!" I whisper.

Prince Azure chuckles, but even with that cocky grin he's wearing, I can see how tired he seems, how frightened. I am sure he wasn't brought here of his own will. King Furlow would not have happily relinquished another of his children to this place.

"Don't curtsy, don't bow," he says. "I think we're well past formalities now." He turns to Nim. "Don't let these girls fool you, what with their dresses and this one's curls. They tried to kill me."

"You were holding us hostage," Pen says through gritted teeth. "Your insane sister kidnapped my betrothed, held a knife to his throat—"

The prince puts his fingers to her lips. "Shh."

Pen's face goes red with rage and I can hear the crack of her knuckles. I put my hand over her fist, a silent plea for her to be calm. She can hit him with another rock some other time. There are more pressing matters to attend to now.

I am trying not to stare at Prince Azure, but I'm so taken aback by the sight of him. When I saw him last, he was limp and lifeless, bleeding from the head and being carried up the stairs by medics. And before that he had been a maniacal, childish young prince scheming with his sister to pry out of Pen and me information about the metal bird that would bring us to the ground.

But like his sister, he has grown since then. "Your Highness," I begin cautiously. "You've surely noticed by now that Internment is in trouble, and we'd like to do what we can to help."

Prince Azure looks to Basil. "It's unfair to be male, isn't it? We're betrothed to these unreasonable things, and for what? Just for being born."

Basil swallows whatever unkind response he'd like to give to that, and instead he says, "Morgan and Pen have some information about Internment that I think you'd be interested in. Perhaps you should ask them what it is."

"They have information about Internment?" Prince Azure says, sneering. "From all the way down here? That's a laugh. I'm the one who's been made to watch as foreigners fly up onto my kingdom in a metal beast of a machine, terrorizing everyone, stealing our soil. I haven't been down here very long"—he looks up at the sky and then sharply back at us—"but the view from down here hardly seems accurate."

Pen is steeling herself beside me, and I fear what she may say next, so I speak first. "Be that as it may, Your Highness"—the honorific is sour on my tongue—"from down here we've been able to see that Internment is sinking."

At that, the prince regards me as though I may be of some use to him after all. "How?" he says. "How can you see that?"

"It was Pen who made the calculations. She was able to compare its location in the sky against the sun. It began sinking bit by bit when the jet started to make its comings and goings."

I don't think I am doing the explanation any justice. I lack Pen's finesse. But the prince seems to believe me. He advances on Pen and says, "How much has it sunk?"

"Not terribly much," she says with surprising civility. "Equal to about an arm's length, which isn't enough to disrupt things. But if the jet keeps passing through the wind surrounding the city, I believe it will weaken the current that helps hold Internment in place. It may continue to sink bit by bit over time, or it may come crashing down all at once. I don't know."

I always thought the prince to be a fool, but he's smart enough to be troubled by all this. He paces with the lantern in his hands. His shadow dances in the fragile light.

"We have to stop the jet," he says. "I already knew that. King Ingram's arrival has brought nothing but chaos to Internment, but if what you say is true, we will have to stop him soon."

Pen looks startled by this. "You believe me?" she says.

The prince stops pacing and looks at her. "By the time I woke up, after you'd hit me, you were long gone. My sister had disappeared, too, and I knew that she had found her way to that contraption of yours that was headed for the ground. I was alone, bedridden, with nothing but free time. I wanted to know everything I could about the girls who'd tried to kill me. The girls my sister had followed to the ground." He waves his hand at me. "You were boring, Stockhour. Yes, your brother was a jumper, but you were as dull as dirt. A nobody."

I know it isn't meant to be a compliment, but somehow I

am flattered that my attempts to blend in and hide my daydreams convinced someone up there.

The prince turns on Pen. "But you, Atmus. The daughter of the top engineer at the glasslands. A perfect student. You have the lights on up in your head, don't you? You're just like your father. A budding engineer."

"I'm not like him," she says feebly. "Having a brain in my head doesn't make me like him."

He narrows his eyes at her. "But you know things. You figure them out. Who else in this bloody world down here would have thought to calculate Internment's position in the sky? Nobody but you."

Pen has nothing to say to this. People who figure things out on Internment are likely to end up dead for treason. If her father knows as much as she does, he's not foolish enough to say it aloud while he's in the city.

The other man clears his throat. "Your Highness, we should be getting back before King Ingram notices that you're gone."

"We want to go back to Internment," I say. "The three of us. We want King Ingram to send us under the pretense of helping his cause, and then we want to help your father overthrow King Ingram's men however we can."

The prince gives a sad smile. "You want to help my father? Our world is being drilled apart, bled dry, and my father has been reduced to nothing. He cannot save us."

"So who can save us, then?" I say. "You?"

"No," he says softly. "Not me."

He allows the other man to lead him back toward the

castle. Down here, he is not a prince, but a prisoner.

"Wait!" Nim calls after him. "Your sister, Celeste, is she all right? Is she alive?"

The prince stops but doesn't turn to face us. "Celeste is a silly princess with silly ideas that she can think the way a king thinks. She fancies herself the political sort. But she only ever makes things worse. You would be wise to forget about her."

Nim's shoulders sag with what may be despair or relief, or both. The prince spoke of Celeste as though she were still alive and well, and that's something.

"I can't stand that little nit," Pen mutters.

"But he listened," I remind her.

Nim is staring off into the darkness. The lantern has been blown out, and the prince and his escort have disappeared from view. Even in the frail bits of moonlight, I can see the pain in Nim's eyes.

"Are they twins?" he asks. "Celeste and her brother."

"No," Pen says. "But they are equally annoying."

"Stop," I whisper to her.

She softens. "Don't let what he said get to you," Pen says to Nim. "You'll see her again. You can try to come back to Internment with us."

Nim shakes his head. "I can't leave Havalais. Someone will have to keep an eye on things here once you've gone. I don't trust my father, or the king."

Two kings who can't be trusted. What a fabulous predicament we're all in now.

We walk back to the hotel, all of us silent, knowing there are no words that could reassure any of us.

5

It's a week before Jack Piper returns home. Nimble plays a contrite role that is painful to watch, but it pays off. He convinces his father that we could be of some help to the king.

Jack Piper, whether it is arrogance or exhaustion, mistakes our scheme for gratitude for Havalais's hospitality. Over dinner he tells us that he's arranged a meeting with King Ingram in the morning.

I stare at my plate, trying to ignore Judas's and Amy's stares. True to my promise to Pen, I have not told anyone about our encounter with the prince. Not even Alice or my brother.

If things go as I hope, I'll tell Lex that I'm leaving. He may wish to stop me, but he won't be able to. He knows that he owes me that much, after letting me think our father was dead. I have to try to find my father as well.

Thomas clears his throat. "Pen?" he says. "Can I speak with you privately?" His calm tone is a mirage.

"It'd be rude to leave the table before dinner is over," Pen says, mirroring his tone.

Basil and I exchange worried glances but say nothing.

When the Pipers begin clearing the dinner plates, I have never been so relieved in my life as I leave that dinner table. Pen, poised and cool, follows Thomas outside. Basil and I go upstairs.

Once we're in my room, I close the door behind us and drop onto the edge of my bed.

Basil sits beside me. "That's going to be an ugly fight the two of them have."

"I wish she had just told him," I say. "He would have been happy. He wants her to go home. He begged me to find a way to get her back to Internment."

"Unless she means to go without him," Basil says.

"I believe that's it," I say. "She's forever evading him. It's been that way since we were children."

"They'll work it out eventually," Basil says. "They always do."

I think of Pen's drawing, the ugly word she wrote over and over on that scrap of request paper, and I wonder if I will ever fully understand her. I wonder if she would want anyone to.

And am I any better than she is? I've got secrets of my own. Even now, the words are on my tongue: Basil, I kissed Judas.

I almost say it. I let it replay in my head over and

over as this loaded silence exists between us.

But I don't. Selfishly I rest my head on his shoulder and I think about the jet breaking through Internment's atmosphere. I think about what will await us when we arrive, if we arrive, and I wonder if any of it can be undone.

Pen is gone for most of the evening, and she returns just as I'm turning down the covers. I'm only going through the motions; I know I'll be too nervous to sleep.

"Well, that was brutal," she says, and falls onto her bed.

"What happened?"

"He was upset that I didn't clue him in to what's going on. It's just that he worries about me, and I feel how much he worries about me." She squirms against the mattress. "All his doting can make me so itchy."

"Did he go along with it?" I say.

"Ultimately, yes. He hates this world. Maybe he's foolishly hoping that we can go back to Internment and it will be as we left it. I don't know." She wriggles under the blanket. "He's going to try to come with us if the king will allow a fourth. I suppose I owe him at least that much."

"Mind if I turn out the lights?"

She shakes her head, closes her eyes.

It's only after I've gotten into my bed and we've settled into the darkness that I'm brave enough to say what's on my mind.

"Do you think I'm a detestable person for kissing Judas?"

"From what I saw, he was the one who kissed you."

"Even so."

I hear the sheets rustling as she moves. "You're not a detestable person, Morgan. I mean, if you were—what does that make me? I'm sure if we kept a tally of our sins, I would be in the lead."

"It's not the quantity of sins in this instance, but the magnitude."

"I don't think it was right," she admits. "But I know you, and I know you wouldn't have done something like that at home. It's this mad world that's made us all feverish."

I think of the night I saved Judas from the patrolmen who were coming for him. I pushed him into the lake to hide him, and after that he tried to scare me off. I still remember the fresh grief in his eyes, the severe angles of his face. He was nothing at all like Basil, and yet he stood so close to me that I could feel his breath. I was terrified with intrigue.

But Pen is right. I wouldn't have kissed him, because back home I did all I could to follow the rules, to be what was expected of me.

"I spent my life thinking all those little things mattered back home. Those rules. But five minutes in this world and it all came undone."

"Stop punishing yourself," Pen says. "Everything I ever loved about you is still intact. I'm sure Basil feels the same way."

We don't speak after that, and eventually her breathing changes, and somehow she has found a way to sleep.

I'm still lying awake when the sun begins to lighten the sky. Nimble knocks on the door and says, "Ten minutes."

It's still early enough that the rest of the house is sleeping. The night's insects are still singing.

Nimble is waiting for us at the door, weaving the car keys between his fingers anxiously. He watches as Pen, Basil, Thomas, and I convene before him. His eyes are sympathetic. "Sorry, kiddos. The king sent word this morning that he'd like to speak with only you and you." He nods to Basil and me.

"What?" Pen says. "But I thought—"

"Prince Azure's request," Nim says. "We should be grateful that he convinced King Ingram to meet with you at all."

Pen looks from Thomas to me, fury in her eyes. "That royal terror is trying to ruin everything."

"He must have a plan," I say, trying to calm her. "Let Basil and me go. We'll see what it's all about, and I'll tell you everything once I return."

Her teeth are gritted, but she knows no good would come from arguing and she gives in.

Nimble is our driver, and as usual, Jack Piper is nowhere. "I visited with Birds yesterday," Nim says, trying to sound cheerful to lighten the mood. He glances at us in the rearview mirror. "Father finally got around to visiting her, and wouldn't you know, they spent the whole time arguing."

"Why?" Basil asks.

"She's got scars," Nim says. "In particular, this deep continuous gash that runs down the side of her face and her arm. Father says it ruins her. He says no man will ever marry her and that he'd like to send her overseas to this surgeon in the north who can fix it. Only, she doesn't want it fixed. She wants to keep it. She says it's a part of her now."

"She should keep it, then," I say.

"Father hates the reminder. I dare even to say that he feels guilty for what's happened to her. Maybe he has a conscience in there after all."

Like burials, this is another custom I don't understand. We wear our scars where I come from.

I meet his eyes in the mirror for an instant before he looks back to the road. "If that's what it's about, don't let him send her off to that surgeon," I say. "If her scars remind him of what he did, he should have to look at them every day. Maybe it will change his mind the next time he goes along with the king's warfare."

"It's a nice thought, but nothing can change his mind once he's made it up. Especially not when he's working for the king." He glances at me in the mirror again. "What's your king like?"

"Celeste didn't talk about him?"

"She did," Nim says. "But with a sort of hopefulness. I got the sense that she was idealizing things when she said he could be reasoned with."

The king's castle has begun to emerge from the distance, and I'm getting a queasy feeling in my stomach.

"Whatever you do," Nim says, "don't let on to the king that you know anything about the phosane. He doesn't think much of broads anyway, so all you have to do is act dense. You don't know anything. You just want to help."

That shouldn't be hard. King Ingram makes me so uneasy that it's hard to speak around him anyway. Maybe it's a good thing Pen isn't here; she isn't intimidated by anyone.

It's a perfectly sunny day, but when we reach the castle, it doesn't glimmer as much as it has in the past. A shadow seems to loom over it.

Nimble brings the car to a stop. He turns in his seat and looks between Basil and me. "Say as little as you can," he says. "Be dumb. If the king realizes you know more than he does about the city sinking, you'll never get what you want. You'll be trapped here working for him."

Two of the king's guards have been waiting for us, and they open the car doors so we can step out.

"King Ingram and his guest are expecting the three of you," a guard says. "Right this way."

I have come to hate this castle. The waste of it. How many bricks were laid, and how much money went into this sprawling palace filled with empty rooms? On Internment, children dream about whether castles exist. I used to dream as well. But in my grandest dreams, the castle was not half the size of this one, and every room was filled with parties and food and dancing girls in sweeping dresses, not a gleaming stone gone to waste.

I'm grateful that Basil is here beside me. When I begin to feel that I'll drown in this world and its strange luxuries, he makes me remember who I am, where we come from.

"You're here, you're here!" King Ingram is clapping as he greets us in the hallway. He walks straight to me and takes my hand in both of his and kisses my knuckles with enthusiasm. "Now I've seen your brilliant little kingdom for myself. It's magnificent!"

"Thank you," I manage, startled by his energy.

"And your friend the princess was kind enough to give me the grand tour. Your people were so happy for her return that there were parties daily. Parades. A marvelous festival."

The only celebration we have on Internment is the Festival of Stars in December, and it both worries and intrigues me to think of the celebration he's describing. King Furlow must have been frightened if he was willing to expend the city's resources to throw such an affair.

But when I realize that King Ingram is waiting for me to speak, what I say is, "And how is Princess Celeste?"

Nimble stands beside me now, and I see his face come alive at the mention of her name, but he quickly hides within himself before the king might notice.

"The poor thing has taken ill. The festivities were a bit much for her. But she is back at home in her charming clock tower castle getting the rest she needs. The journey back to Havalais would have been too much for her, but she sends her love. And I've brought a surprise for all of you, sent from your King Furlow himself."

King Ingram leads us to his parlor, saying "Come, come!" as he goes, like a child excited to receive a gift rather than a king about to give one.

He throws open the heavy wooden doors, and Prince Azure rises up from the wing chair. He is dressed in the fashions of this world: a plaid sport jacket with a silk hand-kerchief in his pocket, and gray pants with sharp creases. But even in the foreign fashion, something about his posture makes me think of home.

"May I present to you Prince Azure of Internment," King Ingram says.

Basil and I feign surprise. He nods into a bow, I into a curtsy.

"Your Highness," Nim says. "Welcome to Havalais."

"Such formality!" King Ingram says. "It's nice to see young people with a regard for custom. Refreshing. But please sit. Sit!"

I sit on the same couch cushion as I did the very first time I met the king, Basil at one side and Nimble at the other.

It has been mere hours since I saw Prince Azure, but he looks the worse for wear. Or perhaps it's only that the lantern light concealed his true condition. He is pale, with light purple bags under his eyes that have been dabbed over with cosmetics. He seems smaller in the daylight, regal but still frail. His hair has grown a bit longer, and a lock of it is doing little to conceal a series of pink scars at his right temple.

He meets my eyes but offers neither a smile nor a frown. A politician's neutral gaze, so much like his father. "I've heard quite a bit about this world, and I'm glad for the opportunity to see it myself," he says.

"Yes, yes, we have quite the itinerary planned," King Ingram says. "Tomorrow afternoon, we'll be presenting our Prince Azure to the rest of the kingdom. My staff is already at work organizing the festivities. There will be radio announcements broadcast today at the top of every hour."

"Plans?" Nimble says.

The king looks to Basil and me. "Well, yes, of course. Our Havalais has fallen on some dark times, I think you'd agree.

60

Warfare, bombings, deaths, and devastation. Of course the phosane mining will fix that, and soon enough peace will be restored. That's all well and good, isn't it? But all of that is a lot to take in, and the people will need a bit of a morale boost, yes? Someone to cheer for."

"Morgan and Basil have expressed a willingness to help, of course," Nim says. "Father said he spoke with you about that."

"Yes, yes, of course, and I'm so glad. And I know just how they can help." King Ingram reaches out and grabs Basil and me each by the left hand, and holds up our ring fingers like a pair of identical trophies. "Love," he whispers excitedly. "It's the biggest thing our two worlds have in common. You two are the perfect representatives for your world. You are young, vibrant, hopeful, in love. You're a prime example of what life on your floating city is all about."

My mouth and throat have gone dry, and I can see my hand paling in the king's grasp. On the surface, he's correct. Basil and I have always been what we were expected to be. Basil still is. I'm the one who has strayed. I'm the one who daydreamed about the edge and admired the sharp angles of another boy's face and throat in the moonlight. I'm the one who has left the pair of us in limbo, wondering what we are and what we will be.

The king releases our hands, and we withdraw.

Nimble senses our trepidation and does the asking for us. "What is it they're expected to do?"

"Well, obviously the pair of you will not be involved in anything dangerous. No. You'll only be asked to appear before a crowd, read a few prepared speeches, and smile."

"We'd be honored," Basil says, without any resentment at all. I'm proud of him for that. I know how much he hates the king; I saw it in his eyes after the bombing at the harbor. It is the same hatred he has for our own king, who has taken the same liberties with the lives of his own citizens. This whole ordeal has made us all quite wary of kings.

But if Basil can fake it, so can I. If wearing a pretty dress and speaking some pretty words will keep us all safe, I will happily oblige. We're getting off quite easily, I think.

And then King Ingram says, "And after the festivities here, the pair of you will return home."

I open my mouth to speak, but words don't form. I can only try to subdue the alarm that is surely washing over my face. Only the two of us?

Basil is once again the steady one. "We're going back to Internment?"

"You'll meet with my father," Prince Azure says. "You'll oversee the phosane mining and speak to the workers."

I look at Prince Azure and just for a moment I see it—a glimmer of fear in his eyes. Worry. Dread. He, too, is a captive of King Ingram.

But it is not safe to ask my questions, and I may never have all my answers anyway. What I do know is that Basil and I are in for something much bigger than festivities. And home will not be as we left it.

King Ingram's staff works quickly. By the time we make the drive back to the hotel, the capital city of Havalais is already hanging banners welcoming the Sky Prince. A stage is being set up before the library.

I look away, down at my betrothal band. It is made of glass and a bit of the phosane this world so desires. It is identical to all the other betrothal bands on Internment. I wonder at the factory worker who crafted this exact ring. That person would never have dreamed what trouble a little ring could cause.

Tears threaten in my eyes and I force them away. Now is not the time to show weakness. I make myself feel nothing.

The driver brings us to the front door, and I do not want to get out of this car. I do not want to face Alice and my brother, and especially Pen, to tell them that I will be returning home without them, and I do not know for how long, and I do not know if I will be back.

Nimble exits the car first, and then he opens the door for me, and reluctantly I step out into the calm, tepid air.

He pats my shoulder in some small gesture of reassurance. "I'm going to walk into the city and visit with Birdie," he says. "I'll tell her you said hello?"

I smile. That does lift my spirits a little. "Yes. Thank you."

"Attagirl," he says. "See you later."

"We don't have to go inside," Basil says once we're alone. "We could stay out here for a little longer."

I look at him. "We got what we wanted, didn't we? I should be happy."

"It's still rather a shock to hear it. And I know that you were expecting Pen to come along." He glances at the sky and then back to me. "I've spent all these months trying to decide if I'd go back, given the chance. It was foolish of me to think I'd have a choice. That any of us would."

"You'll get to see your parents and brother again," I offer, trying to be optimistic. But I worry the words sound bitter. My own mother is gone, and I have no way of knowing whether my father is still alive, or if he's being tortured by the king for his treason.

"Whatever we face, we'll get through it," is all Basil says.

"I'm not scared to go home," I say. It's the truth. Whatever dread I might harbor for that jet ride back home is less than the anticipation and the not knowing. "It's Pen I'm worried about. I've got to go in there and tell her I'm going to leave her behind."

Basil has nothing to say to this. He has always had words of comfort for me in the past, no matter how bad things were, and no matter how undeserving I may have been of his patience at the time. But for this one thing there are no words of comfort.

Tears threaten again. I ball my hands into fists and I refuse to let them free. I take a deep breath. "Best to get this over with, then," I say, and climb the steps and push open the door.

6

Everyone is in the lobby with questions for us. Everyone but my brother, who never leaves his room, and Pen.

Basil offers to tell everyone what's happened, freeing me to look for Pen so that I might speak to her alone.

I find her upstairs on her bed, staring at one of Birdie's old catalogs.

"These drawings are magnificent," Pen says without looking up. She traces the outline of a plumed hat. "They could almost be images. I'm envious of the realism."

"I much prefer your drawings," I say. "Pen?"

She turns the page.

"Pen, there's something I need to speak to you about."

"I will say I don't understand all the plaids," she says. "It's all the men wear. It gets boring. Do they not see that? Back home I always thought Thomas looked more handsome in pinstripes. Well, not handsome, but, you know—acceptable."

I sit on the edge of her bed, and she winces. "Pen."

She closes the catalog and places her hands down on the cover, as though she is trying to keep something trapped within the pages. With difficulty, she says, "What is it?"

Now it's my turn to look at the cover of the catalog in her lap. The drawing of the woman is lifelike. She has dark lips and white teeth, and she's wearing a coat that looks three sizes too big, with pockets big enough to smuggle melons. But in her own way she's glamorous, without a care, much like the Piper children's mother hiding behind the cemetery trees at Riles's funeral. "Do you think Birdie would mind if I kept that?" I ask.

In answer, Pen tosses it into my lap.

"Thank you," I say. I trace my index finger from corner to corner. "Pen, King Ingram is sending Basil and me back to Internment alone."

She is very still, the way she gets some nights when Thomas looks in on her and she pretends to be sleeping. After a moment she reminds herself to breathe, as though waking from a trance, and it's a sharp painful sound.

"I knew it was going to be that," she says.

"He means to use Basil and me as war symbols. He thinks people in Havalais and Internment will be more trusting of two young people in love. He thinks it will give everyone something to hope for."

"Are you in love now?" Pen says. "That's news to me."

"I don't know. That isn't the point."

"Isn't it?" she says coolly. "If two kingdoms are going to rest their hopes on two young people in love, shouldn't they be in love?"

"I love Basil, you know that I do."

"But that's not quite the same thing as being in love, is it?"

I press my lips together, hard. I don't want to fight with her.

I don't think Pen wants to fight either, and in the silence that falls between us, I feel her anger melting away. "When will you leave?"

"The king is planning festivities this week for Prince Azure's arrival. I suspect it will be after that."

"When will you be back?"

"He didn't say."

"Will you be back?"

I don't want to say the words, but I have to, not just for Pen, but for myself, so I can accept what is happening. "I don't know."

There is no color left in Pen's cheeks, no life in her eyes. There was a single day back on Internment when I disappeared and she was told I was dead. She was broken when I found her again, but this is worse than that. She betrays no signs of life now, save for a bottom lip that has begun quivering.

"You know that all of this young-lovers nonsense is a lie King Ingram is telling you and the rest of the two kingdoms," she says.

"Yes," I say.

"You know that he's probably done something horrible to the princess. Maybe she's even dead."

Sickness in my stomach. "Yes. I know."

Her voice cracks. "You know that whatever he's done to the princess to make her disappear, he's going to do the same to you and Basil."

"We're not going to play this game," I say. "We're just going to see what happens."

"No, you'll see what happens. I'll be down here wondering. I'll always wonder and I'll never know if you're hurt, or—or dead, or—"

"Or perfectly fine. Stop it."

There are tears glittering in her eyelashes, and she draws one quick breath after another. I grab her hands, clammy, ice cold. It takes all my strength not to fall apart too, not because of what horrors may or may not await me in the sky, but because I don't want to leave her on the ground in this state.

She nods at the floor. "Okay," she says. "Okay, this is what we wanted, isn't it? A way to go back. So I wasn't invited. You'll just have to cause a big enough commotion for the both of us."

I smile at her. "There's my girl," I say. "See? It will all work out. You and I can go over all of your notes. I'll memorize as much as I can. They can't confiscate plans that are in my head, yes? And whatever happens up in the sky, Basil and I will handle it."

There's a knock on the open door, and Pen turns away, sniffling.

"Hey." It's Judas, standing on the threshold. "Did I come at a bad time?"

"It's always a bad time in this awful place," Pen says.

"I just heard about the king's plans to send you back," he says. He's looking right at me. "I wanted to make sure you were okay. That's all."

Pen laughs incredulously. "You really have some nerve," she says. She gets to her feet and paces out of the room, making a big show of avoiding him as she passes through the doorway.

"Sorry," I say, even though I understand Pen completely. As far as we've fallen from home, she still believes in our traditions. She may think less of me for it, but she still disapproves of Judas taking the liberty to kiss me. Down here in this world, sins are contagious, but someone from home should know better.

A frown tugs at the corner of his mouth. "Be careful, okay?" he says. "Be more than careful. Be clever. Be aware. This king is no more a friend to you than the one who had you poisoned."

I nod. "I know, and Basil knows it, too."

I drop my eyes to the catalog in my lap. I will keep it with me when I go home, a token of this world. Maybe I'll be able to show my father and tell him of the things I've seen.

It hurts to let myself hope.

Judas stands there for a long time. "I wanted to say good-bye."

My heart is pounding. "I'm not leaving yet. There will be time for good-byes later, I'm sure."

"I wanted to say it now. Sometimes you think you'll get a chance later, but then you don't."

I understand. Daphne. And now he's got me thinking about the enormity of all this. Leaving. Possibly never coming back. All the good-byes I have the opportunity, but not the courage, to say. I push it all down, away, out of sight. It's the only way I can bear to keep myself breathing.

But there is one thing I'm bold enough to ask, since I may never get another chance. I look at Judas. "Do I remind you of her? Is that it?"

"Is that it?" he retorts, offended.

"Is that why you kissed me? Is that why you always look at me when you think I'm not paying attention?"

"No, it's not—" He lowers his voice to a whisper, steps into the room. "No it's not why I kissed you. Does there have to be a reason?"

"Customarily when you kiss a person, there is a reason, yes."

Judas shifts his weight uncomfortably. He is tall and thin, and always seems astonished by his limbs, as though he finds the very concept of having a body perplexing. "I don't want you to think I betrayed Daphne," he says. "It isn't like that. She would want me to go on living. She would be proud to know I was defying betrothal laws after her death, rather than dooming myself to never feel anything for another person again. And it isn't that you remind me of her at all. It wasn't about her. She wasn't there. In that moment it was just you."

I'm finding it difficult to breathe. All this time, I felt

certain that Judas's attraction to me was brought on by the madness of being alone. He still mourns her; I know he does.

"I didn't expect that to be your answer," I manage.

"Please believe me, if you never believe another word I say."

"I do. It's just, I—" I clear my throat, turn myself on the bed so that I'm away from him. But that doesn't ease the anxiety or the guilt. It doesn't make this any easier, and I know that I must face him. I stand and take a few steps toward him. "While Daphne may not have been in that moment, Basil was." I press my hand against my chest. "He's very much a part of me. I can't betray him. I won't. Not again."

Judas is looking into my eyes, and I question what I've just said. Was Basil with me in that moment? The real truth is that everything in the worlds fell away. He kissed me, but I kissed back. And now, if he cares for me at all, he will go along with my lie. He will let me pretend that there is nothing between us, until one day it's the truth.

"Okay," he says. Scratches the back of his head. Turns for the door. "Just—okay."

As he crosses the threshold, I say, "Good-bye, Judas."

He pauses, his back to me. Then he walks away without a word. He has already said good-bye.

In the span of a single day, everything has begun to fall apart. I spend much of the day outside, avoiding every-body. And it's only when I'm alone in one of the teacups at the empty amusement park that I allow myself at last to cry. I lie back, sobbing, and stare at Internment's pale purple form in the cloudless sky. I sob for my mother, whose body was likely burnt in secret with all the other victims of the king, without a proper send-off and without anyone to say so much as a few final words. Is her spirit still trapped there, looking for my brother and me? Does she wonder why we've left her?

It is not a pain I've allowed myself to feel. I was so caught up in the danger and the mystery of our journey. I have worn this cloth of grieving tied around my wrist all this time—it is tattered and dirtied—but I have not truly grieved.

Now it comes all at once.

And my father—I have to believe he's alive and whole and safe. I have to.

I shall have to speak to Thomas about Pen. She and I have never been apart for more than a day, and I've seen what loss can do to her. I don't want to return to the ground and find that she has drunk herself into illness. That's what I'll tell Thomas. Make sure she isn't hoarding bottles. Make sure she isn't going off alone. She can be quite deceitful, so be vigilant. I want to see her well when I get back.

When I get back.

That's what I'll say.

7

The festivities are a blur. The king's seamstress and tailor have created clothes for Basil and the prince and me that are a mix of what we wore back home and what people wear in Havalais.

Prince Azure goes up to the podium before us, and he reads the words that have been prepared for him in neat typewritten letters on small squares of paper. Words about joining the kingdoms and ending the war with Dastor. But it is not Prince Azure's war, and it is not Internment's war, and I know that there is anger behind the prince's dazzling smiles.

I never get a chance to ask him about that anger. Nor do I get a chance to ask why he has denied Pen her chance to go to Internment with me. She is the one with the knowledge he needs. The moment after his speech, he is whisked off into the crowd, escorted by two of King Ingram's men, to reassure the people.

Charming the people is nothing new for Prince Azure. Back on Internment there was little else for him to do in public. He is tall and attractive and rather eloquent, even if all his words have been prepared for him.

I sit up on the stage, holding Basil's hand, doing my best not to look terrified.

Eventually the king sends us out into the crowd. He has not given us an exact script, but we know what he wants us to say. Everything will be well. Internment is happy to help. The war will be over soon. Dastor is the enemy but soon they'll leave us alone, once the phosane makes us the more powerful kingdom.

The others don't approach us. Pen and Judas and Amy and Nim. But I see them sometimes in the crowd, watching Basil and me. I see Judas's expressionless face that hides so much, and I see Pen's worried eyes.

I swallow a lump in my throat, and I go on speaking lies.

On our last night in Havalais, Basil and I arrive at the castle for a feast being held in our honor. A send-off. Roasted animals of every variety and vegetables that weren't cut out of a can, for once in this world. I force myself to eat. Everything tastes like paste. All I want is to go home, and I'm not sure where that is anymore.

"Ghastly party, isn't it?" Prince Azure says, stepping up from behind me. He's holding two long-stemmed glasses of sparkling tonic and he hands one to me. "I think that's an entire pig on that table over there with—what is that in its mouth?"

"I don't know," I say, because I'm too nauseated to look.

"Tomorrow's the big day," the prince says. "I have been waiting all week to have a moment alone with you. Looks like now's our only chance." He nods to the opened glass doors that lead to the balcony.

I look to Basil, trapped in a conversation between the king and one of his guests.

"Hurry, before the king forces us to recite another line from one of his scripts." Despite his glibness, I can hear in his tone that he's serious, and I let him lead me onto the balcony.

The hot and humid air is hardly better than that of the stale party, but Prince Azure seems relieved. He pauses for a moment to breathe it in.

"So that was him?" Prince Azure says. "That boy with the glass over his eyes? The one my sister is so in love with?"

"Nimble Piper," I say. "That was him."

Prince Azure huffs. "I expected something more extraordinary, to hear the way she spoke on about him. He hardly seems like a prince, although I'll hand it to him, he is doing a brilliant job concealing his lineage."

"For what it's worth, he's kind," I say.

Prince Azure stares out at the sky. "That is worth something."

"Is Celeste—is she all right?" I say.

"She's taken ill," Prince Azure says. "She was in no condition to be flying between worlds. King Ingram meant to drag her to Havalais anyway, but Father put his foot down and sent me instead."

"But she's alive," I think aloud.

Prince Azure throws me a frosty glare. "Yes. And she had all manner of kind things to say about you. For that and so many other reasons, I think the ground caused her to go mad."

"Is that why you've advised the king to send Basil and me back to Internment?" I say. "Pen would be valuable to Internment, and if you're trying to keep her down here out of spite—"

"I am trying to keep her alive," he says. "Do I care for her? No. She tried to kill me and I don't especially like what she does with her hair. But her value is not lost on me. I know that she is the one who figured it all out about the phosane, or as we call it back home, sunstone. I know that she has an engineer's head on her shoulders. And if my father knew this, she'd be on her way to the clock tower as soon as you touched ground, and she would spend what's left of her life there, working for him."

"Pen would never," I say.

"She would, or she would be tortured. Drowned within a sliver of death. Cut. Hung by her wrists."

I force the imagery from my mind and keep my steady gaze on him. "Is that the sort of torture you saw at the attraction camp? For people who are attracted to the same sex?"

He pales at that. Swallows a hard lump in his throat and goes on, "When King Ingram asked which one of you should be used as symbols, I chose the pair of you because of your dumb expressions. Look at you—you're utterly harmless. Nobody would suspect you had a valuable thought in your head. But that friend of yours is another story. My sister told me all about how brilliant she is and on this front, I believe her."

"Why did you choose me, then? If you want to save Internment so badly and Pen's so valuable?"

Prince Azure closes his eyes for a long, painful moment. "Because I do not want her helping my father. Or King Ingram. I no longer believe either of them can do what's best for Internment."

"We agree, then," I say. "Your father is doing more harm than good."

Prince Azure waves his hand. "Fine. Let's be candid. Yes, I agree with you. My father's way may have been sinister at times, but it worked when Internment was self-contained. He had people killed in the interest of suppressing riots that would have destroyed the city. But now things have changed. I need you and that betrothed of yours to go up there with your dumb expressions and play the part of two harmless idiots. I need you to talk to my sister. She'll know what needs to be done. And moreover, I need you to look after her."

I blink. "I thought you were coming back with us."

"You don't get it, do you?" he says. "I'm not here by choice, Stockhour."

King Ingram has spotted us, and from across his party he calls our names, waving us enthusiastically back into the party.

I follow after Prince Azure, with a lead anchor in the pit of my stomach.

When I return to the hotel, I fall into bed without bothering to unpin my hair or scrub the cosmetics from my skin.

Pen climbs into the bed with me and for the longest time we don't speak. My back is turned to her, and I'm watching the curtain arch around the open window like a force field when the wind comes.

"I've been thinking about the gardens of stones," she says.

"The graveyards?"

"Yes. Those. I've been thinking about all those bodies beneath the earth just rotting and feeding the worms and the soil. On Internment we burn everything away—the skin and the bones, the brain, the heart, until there's just dust."

She rests her chin on my shoulder. "But down here, what's left inside these people who are buried? Do they still hold on to the secrets that people have told them? Where does it all go?"

"I don't know," I say.

"I think we have a lot in common with the dead," Pen says. "We're filled with things we won't say out loud. Things that get trapped inside us that nobody will ever hear."

When I leave, is she going to go on having thoughts like this? "We aren't dead," I remind her. "What we say or don't say, the secrets we do or don't keep—those are all choices. Conscious choices we get to make while we're alive."

"I thought you'd see it that way." She lies back against the pillow. "If there's anyone I can tell my secrets to, it's you, Morgan. You'll keep them if I ask, won't you?"

"Of course I will."

I understand now what is about to happen. Several months ago, I discovered one of her secrets on a piece of paper that was meant to be burnt at the Festival of Stars. It was the most desperate, hateful thing I'd ever seen her draw: buildings with the word "die" making up their bricks and plumes of chimney smoke. We fought each other to the ground over that bit of paper and she never fully explained what it meant.

That secret has taken on a body of its own. It sits between us all the time, this thing we don't acknowledge.

She turns away from me and settles with the back of her head against mine. "It started the day my father took me to the glasslands," she says. "It was evening and we were alone. He said we were going to share a secret, he and I. I knew that something was wrong, because he'd never so much as talked about his work with me, much less taken me to see it." She is very still as she talks.

I don't understand but I don't ask. I know that if I interrupt, she will stop this story and never begin again. "I don't even remember if I looked at him. I remember the spire filling up with orange light as the sun went down. I remember reciting a poem in my head. You know, the one we read in kinder year about the flowers being the eyes of the god in the sky, spread out to keep watch over us. I recited it over and over until the words didn't seem like words anymore.

"That was the first time."

I close my eyes tight against the words she is about to say.

"After that, he started coming to my bedroom when it was late. Usually just as the sky was changing before the sunrise. I told Mother about it. She was still good back then. She still had her wits. She went right to the clock tower, to speak to one of the king's advisers.

"But what could be done when my father was so important to the glasslands? He's one of their top engineers. He was in the middle of a project to outfit older buildings with electricity. The king didn't want a scandal. So it was decided that I was mistaken, then. I had to speak to a specialist and explain, once a week, why I wouldn't stop telling these lies.

"Do you know what I remember most, though? All the lines that started appearing in my mother's face. You'd think I'd be the one crying about it, but it was never me. It was always her. Breaking into hysterics while she was washing the dishes, or going for these long walks and not returning until after my father had gone to sleep. She never slept herself, and she was prescribed tonic. As much as she wanted. As much as it would take to drown her thoughts."

My nails are digging into my palms, and I hold my breath for long stretches, exhaling slowly, silently. I always blamed Pen's mother for her battle with tonic. Vilified her at times for spreading that toxic addiction to her only daughter like a terminal disease. I never once thought that there might have been a cause.

"There are dozens of men like my father on Internment. Maybe even hundreds. Even if you look, you won't see them. Every king knows what happens in his kingdom. He knows how to hide things. I'm not afraid of my father anymore. I don't know that I ever was. I've been afraid of what would happen to my mother and me if anyone found out.

My mother can't handle herself the way that I can. She's like a train car that only goes backward. Around and around all the time in the wrong direction, and there's nothing I can do to even slow her down. It wasn't always that way, I think, but it has been for as long as I've been alive. I suppose I can't blame my father for all of her madness. I don't believe in that. I don't believe in letting other people be the reason we turn out the way that we do.

"Thomas doesn't know. He absolutely can't. He may not seem like much, but if he found out, I know that he would do something as violent as it is stupid." She's right. The boy has no sensibility when it comes to her, he loves her so. "I've found ways to handle it myself. I've started keeping a knife under my pillow, and the last time he came into my room, I pretended to be asleep until he came close, and then I had the knife at his cheek and I asked him how he would explain his injuries at work tomorrow. He does so value his charming smile. That's how he gets everyone to trust him."

The curtain falls limp as the wind leaves it. Insects impassively go on with their songs.

For the first time all night, Pen's voice loses its cool detachment and she sounds small. "Say something."

Say something.

After Lex's incident I modeled myself after her. I wanted to be as strong for my parents as she was for her declining mother. I foolishly believed that we had something in common, something we didn't have to talk about. Every night while I slept safely in my bed, while my greatest problem was that I didn't have the attention I craved, the light was being stolen from Pen's spirit, and I saw nothing, did nothing. And rather than bonding over our tragic little lives, the real truth was that our childhood was disappearing behind our footfalls as we walked, hand in hand, down very different paths.

"I remember this one December, we must have been seven or eight," I say. "We were at the Festival of Stars. My brother was supposed to come and light our papers for us, but you had been bouncing all day; you had thought of something really important to ask for, and you couldn't wait any longer. So you climbed onto one of the picnic tables so you could reach the flame lantern. I couldn't have stopped you if I'd tried. The fire burnt right down to your fingers before you let the paper go and it spiraled away from you. You stood there in your white dress, the hem and ribbons already stained by the grass, and you watched your flame disappear into a sky that was already on fire."

The sun was deep orange, like it was bleeding into the sky, and everything—our whole world—had seemed ablaze.

"You were beautiful. You were the bravest and most powerful thing in the sky."

I turn to face her in the darkness. The moonlight clings to the curve of her cheek. "I still see that girl when I look at you," I say. "I always will."

Pen closes her eyes, and her stoic expression melts.

"No one has ever seen me the way you do," she says.

8

It's early when Nim knocks at my door. The sun itself is still sleeping. "We'll be leaving in a half hour," he says, and then he's gone. I'm uncertain whether or not I've slept. I didn't dream, and spent most of the night in silence, with Pen just as silent beside me.

I light a candle so I can see what I'm doing, but I don't turn on the light as I slip into a dress from the closet. It's satin with a drop waist, and a sequined collar. The fashion will startle the king, if he bothers to notice.

I thought Pen was sleeping, but she sits up and watches me attempt to brush the tangles from my hair. "I told you not to go to bed with all those pins in it."

"What do you think everyone back home will say about this dress?" I say, and can't help but grin.

"It's positively scandalous," Pen says, dropping back against the pillows with a flourish. Staring up at the ceiling, she says, "Are you nervous about flying in the jet?"

"After tumbling to the earth in the professor's metal bird, it's a relief to be flying in something with a proper engine."

"That bird was quite impressive, though," Pen says. "It had a full kitchen. I think we could have lived there if things had gone differently. For a while, at least."

"You should draw it," I say. "Not like a map, but a full rendition, with the bolts and gears and everything."

"I don't know if I remember it clearly enough now."

"Of course you do. Your mind works that way. You capture images of things and they stay up in your head forever."

She sits up again, turns on the lamp, and looks at me. "I hope you're right."

It's painful to take in the sight of her. Twin braids. Sleepy green eyes. Defiant smirk that never really leaves her lips. I saw it even after her body was pulled from the water, taunting death itself.

She squints curiously at me. "What is it?"

"I'm just thinking is all."

"Yes, thank you, I gathered that much."

Everything has changed. That's what I'm thinking. The way I saw the world has changed. The way I saw life. But Pen still looks the same. My beautiful Pen, who has given me her ugliest secret.

"Do you really want the truth?" I ask.

"Yes, I really do."

"I'm thinking that when I go home, I don't know what will be waiting for me, but I hope that I can find your father—in your apartment or just leaving the glasslands. I'm thinking I'd like to stop his heart. It isn't right. What he did. It isn't right that Daphne and my mother and how many others had to die such awful deaths, but he goes on as though he's done nothing wrong."

Her face softens. Her eyes have awoken now.

"You don't have to kill my father," she says, her voice gentle. "But I can't tell you how much it means to me that someone else wants him gone as much as I do."

"Maybe I'll only trip him, then."

She laughs. It's an explosive laugh, and she throws her hand over her mouth, and in the next instant she's sobbing.

I go to her, sit across from her on the bed. "Don't cry," I say, but my own eyes are filling. "Don't."

"Nothing bad can happen to you, Morgan. Do you understand? There are pieces of me—important pieces— that stop existing when you're not around."

Shuddering, she grabs my hands, but then changes her mind and throws her arms around me.

"When I told the king about the phosane, I was thinking of what would be best for you," I remind her. "So I want to find the same Pen when I return. Sober and alive."

She nods. Furiously, desperately, because she will tell me anything I want to hear in this moment. Anything that will make me happy. It is our way of protecting each other, filling each other's heads with these silly illusions that nei- ther of us will change a drop while we're apart, and that we will see each other again.

When I leave the bedroom, I close the door behind me, holding the knob so as to make as little noise as possible. Most of the house is sleeping, and I'd like to avoid a teary good-bye.

But someone is waiting for me at the top of the stairs.

Alice's hair is bright red even as the rest of her is shadowed by the darkness of the hour. I hold my breath. It is the only way I won't fall to pieces and change my mind about going.

I can just see her sad smile. "I wanted to say good-bye before you left. Lex asked me to wake him, but it seemed for the best if I didn't."

My brother and I had come to an understanding of sorts. He had lied about our father. If I was choosing to return home, he owed me enough to let me go. But he didn't have to like it. If he were standing here now, he would try to stop me, and being my brother and knowing me as he does, he would play to my sympathies. He would know just what to say, not to stop me, but to make me feel lousy enough about going.

"Don't worry," Alice says. "I'll look after him."

"Look after yourself, too," I say, my voice tight. I will miss them both terribly.

"I'm working on him," she says. "I think I've almost convinced him to come around to this world. When this war is through, we can get a new apartment. He can write his novels, I can work."

"Just like home, but entirely the opposite," I say.

She laughs. "Yes."

I take her hands. "Tell him that there are different free-doms down here," I say. "Tell him that no one will stigma-tize him for being a jumper—the people down here don't even know what that is. Tell him you can have a family."

She squeezes my hands. "That one will take more time, love. There's so much healing to do."

"Healing can only happen once you begin the process. Tell him."

"Yes," she says, and her voice cracks with tears. I think it's because I brought up that awful memory again, and I hate myself for being so hasty. I'm so desperate for them to be happy that I lose my own patience. But Alice puts her arms around me, kisses my cheek with such force, I can still feel her lips even after she's drawn back. "Come back to us alive," she says. "Whatever you have to do."

I can't bear another promise I'm not sure I can keep. Instead I hug her and I tell her I love her, and I remind her again to combat Lex's stubbornness and get him to rejoin the living. They're both still so young. I can't stand the thought of my brother squandering all the decades they both have left to live. "There's still a life for you down here," I say. "Don't let him go on harping about the terrible things when there's still so much good."

She hugs me again. There are no more promises to be made, and neither of us wants to say good-bye. When we at last let go, I offer a smile before I turn away and descend the stairs.

Basil is wearing what I think is one of Nim's suits. He looks striking in it, I think, even if the shoulders are a bit snug. Nim is considerably thin and willowy.

Basil gives a somber smile when he sees me. There are tears in my eyes.

"Hi," I say, keeping my voice low. The rest of the hotel is sleeping, or pretending to be asleep. Nimble says we're running a few minutes early. He says we can go say good-bye to the others if we like. "Until next time," he quickly adds.

I look at Basil. "I don't want to. But you should go on if there's anything you need to say."

"What about your brother?" he asks.

I especially don't want to say good-bye to him. If there is anyone in this hotel whose words are powerful enough to change my mind, it's Lex.

Even if my father's death were a certainty, I would go. I still belong to Internment. It's still a part of me. I have to see this through. I want to.

"I've said all my good-byes," I tell him.

Jack Piper is nowhere, nor is his driver. Nim leads us to one of the black cars used by the staff here, and he drives us himself.

We reach a turn in the road, and the hotel is no longer visible when I look back, and I break into a fresh round of tears. They fast become hysterical, and I am a mess of incoherent whimpers that are meant to be the names of the people in that hotel.

Basil puts his arms around me, rubs my back and whispers that it's okay, let it out, go on, I've been incredibly brave. He understands that this is harder for me than it is for him. We are returning to his family and leaving mine behind.

He kisses the crown of my head. "Oh, Morgan."

I shake in his arms the way that Pen shook in mine. I think she was what held me together for so long. "I wanted to be strong for her." I gag on saliva. "And Alice and—" I can't speak.

Basil holds me steady against the jostling of the car. He has to be the steady one when I can't be. Alice was right. Things change. People leave. The one whose blood fills your ring is the one who never leaves your side.

I tighten my fists around his shirt.

For all its hype, the send-off is unspectacular. Nim stops the car in what at first seems to be the middle of a field. Then, in the approaching sunlight, I see the long stretch of concrete that leads like a road to a multilevel building with a large, closed door making up its front.

"Take a minute to dry your eyes," Nim says. "We're running early anyway." He turns in his seat and gives me the handkerchief from his pocket. It's embroidered with a black *JP*, for "Jack Piper." The real name he never uses.

I sniff. "Thank you."

His lips are pressed tightly, not quite a smile. I am going to miss him, and his sisters, but I can't think about that now if there's any chance of holding myself together. I watch him step out of the car and close the door behind him.

I dab at my eyes, blow my nose, and let out a shuddering breath.

"Why didn't you tell me this is how it felt when you left your family behind?" I say.

"It wasn't quite the same." Basil uses his sleeve to dab at my persistent tears. "I knew that I was making the choice they'd want me to make. I knew that their best chance at staying safe was for me to leave them behind."

I shake my head. "This isn't what my brother or Alice want. That's why I couldn't say good-bye to my brother. I want it to seem as though—as though I just stepped out for a walk before he woke up, and I'll be back soon." I look at him. "And Pen. I need her. I need both of you in my life. I don't know who I am without the two of you beside me."

"You're Morgan," he says. "The girl I could never keep up with in kinder year, who was always chasing flutter-lings and even bramble flies—anything with wings. You're the girl who dove into that ocean when Pen didn't surface. You're the thing that calls me back when my thoughts have begun to tread into darkness."

I sniffle dumbly. "I am?"

He tilts my chin so that I'm looking at him. "Yes."

"You always know the exact thing to say." I blow my nose again and fold the handkerchief in my lap. "I don't suppose Nim will want this back."

Basil laughs. "He probably meant for you to keep it."

"Shall we go, then?"

"I'm ready if you are."

Basil opens the door, and I follow him out into the dark morning air. It's chilly, although last night was quite warm.

I hug my arms across my stomach. "Your weather is unpredictable," I say to Nim.

We begin the walk down the concrete, and to keep myself rooted in the moment, I tell Nim about the long seasons and the short back home. There is no real weather. No snow. A slight change in the leaves sometimes, a slight dip in the temperature when the days get shorter, but nothing like this.

"I imagine all of our seasons must be a nuisance for someone like you," he says.

"No. I think they're beautiful."

"What do you call this road?" Basil asks. "It's strange. On one end it just stops in the grass."

"It's a runway," Nim says. "The plane will come out of that carriage house there, and pick up momentum by speeding down the runway, and then it'll take flight."

I turn to him as we walk. "Do you wish you were coming with us?"

"The idea is intriguing," he admits. "But I have my sisters to look after." He brightens a little. "Birds will be excited to know you've gone home. She'll expect all sorts of stories when you return." He says it with such confidence, and I cannot tell whether he believes it himself or is just a convincing liar for my sake.

I play along. "I'm looking forward to seeing her up and about."

I look ahead to see that the carriage house that holds the plane is much closer. I can hear voices echoing inside its brick walls.

"Morgan," Nim says. "Your kindness meant a lot to Celeste. She told me that you were someone she could trust. One of the only people that she could trust, actually. I was wondering if maybe—if you could give this to her. When you see her, that is." He has extracted a folded envelope from his breast pocket and he puts it in my hand. It's sealed shut, and I can feel the heft of several pages inside. "It's very important that she's the only one who reads that."

I meet his eyes. "Of course," I say.

"And if—" He cuts himself off and then begins anew after he's summoned some courage. "And if what the others have feared is true, and she's no longer alive, I need you to destroy that for me."

I'm amazed by his bravery, saying those words and accepting them as a possibility.

"Okay," I say, and repeat something I've heard Birdie say so many times, copying her accent and emphasizing the four syllables. "Absolutely."

Nim smiles, punches my shoulder lightly. "Thanks, kiddo."

He bangs on the wooden door to the carriage house: once, pause, three times, pause, once.

There's a stirring and a metallic sound from within, like ropes being fed through a pulley, and then the door begins lumbering upward, arching back into the carriage house itself.

As the door rises and I begin to get a good look at the jet in the early morning light, a painfully bright flash blinds me. Too late, we shield our eyes. "There they are, our lovely young beacons of hope!" the king says. He's holding a heavy-looking metal device in front of his face, and he lowers it to smile at us. "That will look lovely on the front page of the paper. I'll be sure to reserve a copy for you when you return."

If you don't call upon your men to kill us, I think. That's what my own king tried to do to me.

As the burning dots fade from my vision, I see Prince Azure standing behind the king, outfitted on either side by two of King Ingram's men. *Hostage,* I think. He is dressed in more of this world's fashions; if he were to return home like this, it would take mere seconds for the schoolboys back home to mimic this foreign image. Internment would begin to resemble the ground. The thought frightens me more than I was prepared for.

The prince's weary eyes are on Nim, the boy from a strange land who stole his sister's heart.

Nim notices and tips his cap in greeting, but this gets no response.

Beside the prince, the jet sits like a giant metal creature I'd expect to find in one of the oceans here. If the professor's contraption was a bird, this is a creature of the sea. A whale with an arched back and pectoral fins spread out at either side. The metal is dark with "001" painted on the side in chipped white letters.

I turn to Basil, who is staring at the thing with worried eyes. I'd like to console him, but it doesn't seem wise to speak candidly in the king's presence. And besides that, I don't want to lie to him.

The king positions Basil and the prince and me at the jet's nose for photos. I'm made to stand between the two of them with my arms up around their shoulders. Through his teeth, Prince Azure says to me, "It'll go a lot faster if you smile." He glances at me. "Not like you're facing execution. Like you mean it."

I force my best smile. The king seems pleased with the lot of us and he hands the horrid flashing device to one of his men. They call it a camera, I know, but it's a much more crude version of the image recorders we have back home. This world has many advances compared to Internment, but Internment has much better technology. I suppose Havalais harnessing the phosane would change all that.

"This is the part where I wish you all safe travels," the king says. He hands Basil and me each a thick stack of papers. "I've prepared some notes—scripts, information, itineraries, what to say when you are asked certain questions. There will be someone waiting to receive you when you return home."

Home. He shouldn't be allowed to use such an intimate word to describe the place he's so cheerfully willing to destroy.

His delighted grin does nothing to ease my mind. I am more sure than ever that some horrible fate awaits us back home. He has used us as symbols of hope, and now that we're leaving, he can tell his kingdom all sorts of brilliant stories about what we're doing up there. No need for us to be alive for that.

One of the men opens the jet's door. It unfolds from the body of the jet like a bit of orange peel. Our shoes make hard noises on the metal steps as we climb up to the door. Basil goes first and I follow. Just before I step into the jet's doorway, I look back over my shoulder at Nim, who gives me a pitying smile. Beside him, the prince mouths the words "my sister." I give the slightest of nods so that the king, giddy about his plans, won't see it.

As I step onto the jet, two men wheel away the ladder. Basil grips my arm as though he thinks I might fall in the open space. And then the same two men swing the door shut behind us with a jarring slam. I tense. The jet's shudder never leaves my body, instead running up and down my bones, trapped inside me.

It's dim inside the jet. The only light comes from the rows of small windows on either side of the tiny chamber.

The ceiling is low and arched. Basil can't stand fully upright and must duck his head as we make our way to the seats. The seats are very similar to the ones on the trains back home. There are four of them, made of polished brown leather, in pairs of two that face one another beside a small oval window.

My legs are shaking as I bend into a seat beside the window. Basil sits beside me and puts his hand on my knee.

I notice two buckets under the seats across from us. "What do you suppose those are for?" I say, desperate for a distraction.

"In case we need to get sick," Basil guesses. I don't feel any better. I didn't get sick when we fell out of the sky, but now the thought has been put into my head, and I purse my lips together.

A roar begins from seemingly within the jet's walls. Our seats rattle and shake. I grip Basil's hand that's on my knee. I can feel the last breath he draws before he holds it all in. The jet lurches forward, and the darkness of the garage outside the window becomes the lightening sky. I see Nim with his hands in his pocket for less than a second before he has been ripped from view. The grass flies past us, an endless field, and then suddenly that grass is far below us. We are moving up, leaving my stomach below us.

My hand, squeezing Basil's, is slick with sweat. My face is hot and then cold.

Basil exhales, and his next breaths are shallow and light. He's staring at the tiny window.

I take a deep breath and exhale hard. "Maybe it will distract us if we read these papers King Ingram left with us."

Basil shakes his head lightly. "I can't look at words just now."

I don't think I'm much in the condition for reading, either. I roll my head back against the seat and try to find my bearings.

Several minutes of quiet pass, and as soon as I realize I won't need the bucket under my seat, I do feel better.

We don't speak, either because we fear being sick, or because this week of being paraded about has exhausted us.

An hour into the flight, my head feels as though it were being compressed in a vise. I lean against Basil, who draws patterns on my knee, pausing occasionally to rub the satin of my dress between his fingers.

I think of the grim alternate reality Prince Azure painted for Pen. Shackled and tortured in the clock tower, prodded for information. Her mind has always been a commodity, and I think she's always known it, because she has kept her brilliance hidden. She whispers her secrets aloud only when we're alone. Never trusting anyone. She knew it was unsafe.

And despite trying not to, I think of what Pen endured at her father's hand. I think of all those mornings back home when she dabbed herself with cosmetics or struggled to stay awake on the train and carried the scent of tonic. All those times I held her hair away from her face when she was sick, wondering what this affliction was that caused her to drink as much as she did. How stupid I was, and how useless.

"Are you all right?" Basil asks, leaning forward to see my face.

I nod. Whether I see Pen ever again or not, this is one secret of hers that I will keep. I say, "Prince Azure pulled me aside at the party last night. He's afraid, Basil. He's a hostage."

Basil nods. "King Ingram is using him for some sort of leverage, to be sure."

"Do you think King Ingram will kill him if Internment goes on refusing to comply?" I say.

"It's possible. But if that's the case, do you think he's willing to die for Internment?"

"It wouldn't do much good," I say. "If Internment goes

on being useless to King Ingram's plan, what's to stop him from bombing the entire city right out of the sky?" I stare out the window at wisps of clouds. The ground is a faraway patch of green. "Prince Azure told me to speak to his sister. He didn't have a chance to explain, but I think the two of them have something planned and they seem to think we can help."

"I hope they're right," Basil says. "Resistance is fine and well, but a tiny floating city can avoid a king's wrath for only so long."

Our fingers have become intertwined, and I stare down at his betrothal band, empty of my blood. I wonder if we'll live long enough to speak our vows. I wonder if we will still choose each other if we're given the luxury of that time.

"Look." Basil nods to the window, and I follow his gaze.

There at a distance, floating in the still blue, is a swirling sphere of clouds, a perfect dome. And below that I see the jagged earth, and I realize at once that this is home. A small cloud drifts toward it and immediately gets pulled into the current of wind, zipping into fast motion.

"It always looks so much calmer from within the city," I say.

"It's something, isn't it?" Basil says.

We're approaching rapidly, huddled around that small window as we watch our world from the outside. These clouds are swirling in the wind that threw my brother back against the earth when he got too close. It nearly killed him. Amy too. It changed them irreparably. It killed so many others.

We slice through that wind like through water. The jet wobbles and shakes and I think that surely we will be propelled back into the sky, away from the city, from the force of it.

The jet holds steady, though, and the window fills up with white for a moment before I see dirt.

We touch ground and I can hear the furious squealing of the jet's wheels, and I begin to worry that we'll careen into the train tracks in the distance.

I brace myself, gripping the edge of the seat. Basil's arm, pressed against mine, is so tense, there could be steel under his skin.

When we finally stop, my head and stomach are still speeding off ahead of me somewhere. I can feel myself breathing, but I am not in control of my own body as it struggles to understand that I've stopped flying.

It takes several seconds for me to focus, and when I do, I wish, not for the first time, that Pen were here. She would somehow know exactly where we are.

When my vision settles enough that I can see what's on the other side of the window, I realize that we are just outside the train tracks, on the long stretch of unused land between the tracks and the road. The grass here grows scraggly and wild, scarcely tended to.

I have time to give Basil only a worried look before the door is opened and we're pulled out by a group of King Furlow's patrolmen. I hear a low growl in Basil's throat when one of the guards pulls me down the last step. In an instant Basil is at my side, keeping pace.

I hold nothing but contempt for these patrolmen after what they've done to my family. Which of them are to be trusted? But even as they're telling us to step outside and move quickly, I hear the cadence of their voices—Birdie called it an accent—like my own, and I know that I am once again home.

The air is perfect, warm and still. The sky is calm.

I count five patrolmen, and they lead us over the train tracks, back to within the city's limits. I'd never been on the wrong side of these tracks before, but I no longer fear that being too close to the edge of the city will drive me mad. I have seen madness in a king who would allow an attack on his own city for political gain. I have seen bodies cracked open like fruit fallen from a tree and left to rot in the sun. There's no god in that wind, warning me away or calling me closer.

Even more unnerving are the men in clothes that are not from this world. I recognize the drab gray of their coats. I saw them in the dozens after the explosion at the harbor. Soldiers from King Ingram's army.

I look to the workers ahead of me. I recognize some of them from my section or Basil's. There's a woman who worked as a seamstress and who repaired my coat sleeve when I tore it on a loose scrap of metal jutting from the train's wall. Now she is glistening with sweat. She spears the dirt with a shovel, searching for the clumps of soil that glimmer with that invaluable mineral that can be refined.

With all this open land, we must be in Section Seven, a broad field in which animals are bred and free to roam.

Only, there are no animals here now. The land is being torn apart. Ruined. The grass has started to brown and thin, as though it would rather die than be a part of what's being done here.

The workers all seem to be going out of their way to avoid looking at us. They've been instructed not to, I think.

I look for my father in the crowd. And then I look for his face among the patrolmen standing guard. He is nowhere.

Basil walks in silence beside me, but I note the nearly imperceptible change in his next breath and I follow his gaze. He's looking at a woman who is waist-high in one of the holes, brushing at the dirt with her fingers, looking for specks that will be of use. His mother.

At first I think she hasn't seen us yet. But then she looks at him. Sharpness and longing in her eyes. She goes right back to her task.

I touch Basil's arm to bring him back to me. I fear what will happen to him if he's caught staring, or if any of the guards realize he's related to one of the workers. I do not know what our presence means, if we're hated or loved.

It's hard to think we would be loved.

We walk for what feels like an hour, until the workers are behind us and we eventually come to a cobblestone road. There aren't many shuttles in this section, nor is there a train platform nearby—it would startle the livestock. There is a shuttle bus waiting for us here now, though. The patrolmen guide us inside.

It's just Basil and me, and a patrolman who stands by the door, watching us even as the shuttle begins to move.

The man driving the shuttle is dressed in the gray of King Ingram's soldiers.

We are all silent, but I know Basil. I look at his face and I can see that something has changed. The sight of his mother working with the mining effort, unable to so much as speak to him, has proven to us that things are not as we left them.

I don't ask where we're going. We drive on the outskirts of Section Seven, far from any buildings. I never knew Internment had so many trees. I never knew the section for livestock was so vast. We could almost be on Havalais, I think. I've become accustomed to the idea that a patch of land can go on forever, never stopping at all, but rather looping back around to itself.

When I begin to recognize where we are, my skin prickles. Through the window I can see the clock tower in the distance.

"Out," the patrolman says after the shuttle has come to a stop.

As I follow Basil down the aisle, my body thinks, for just a moment, that I am moving for the train that will take us to school. It is a normal day. It is all the same inside the shuttle—the metal walls, the cushioned seats, the smell of it. It is the same and not the same.

A train hasn't gone by since we landed. Even this far from the tracks, I would still be able to hear it. I would still feel the rattle under my feet. One surely should have passed by now.

It's been hours since we left Havalais, and I force myself not to think of what the others might be doing on the ground now that they're surely awake. But the clock tower does not make for a pleasant distraction.

Nim's letter to Celeste sits heavily against my chest, where I've folded it in half and tucked it under my dress for safekeeping and to hide it. As unique and glamorous as the fashions of the ground are, women's clothing in particular isn't very practical. If I were wearing my uniform or one of my old dresses, there would be pockets. There would be more modesty as well.

I'm feeling very conscious, suddenly, of the short hem of this dress, the straps that do nothing to cover my shoulders. This feeling only intensifies when we reach the clock tower and I realize that we are surely on our way to see King Furlow.

The main floor of the clock tower is a public lobby. I was here a few times with my parents when they were collecting their weekly wages, and once on a tour in first year. The last time Alice was here was when she appealed directly to the king about allowing the birth of her child. After that, neither she nor Lex could stand to come back, and I would often collect their wages for them so they wouldn't have to.

I find myself once again looking for my father. But he isn't here; hardly anyone is. Most of the citizens must be out there mining for fuel. Internment has become a labor camp, just as we all feared.

Two patrolmen lead us down a hallway that's always restricted from the public, and it leads to a single door I've never seen. The door is unlike the others on Internment. Rather than wood, it is made of steel. There are two locks above the doorknob, and each patrolman holds just one of the keys to open it.

The door opens, revealing an archaic staircase made of carved stone. Parts of the steps have crumbled into pebbles, and I can tell the staircase has never been repaired and is probably as old as the clock tower itself.

We move single file, with a patrolman ahead of us and a patrolman behind us, for what seems to be a thousand steps spiraling up the walls of the clock tower.

When at last we reach a landing, one of the patrolmen stands to attention while the other unlocks the door. I wonder if there has always been this much security surrounding the king, or if this is all in light of the hatred he must be facing for what Internment has become.

The patrolman moves through the open door, and looks over his shoulder at us. "Come on, then," he says. "The king will be expecting you."

I'd like to take hold of Basil's hand, but I don't dare. Neither of us betray fear or emotion of any kind as we step forward, clutching only the stack of instructions King Ingram doled out to us this morning.

No wooden floor covers the original stone of this tower, and our footsteps and breaths echo as we move. We pass several closed doors along the wall, and then, at last, we come to the end of the hallway, and the patrolman opens a final door.

When I last saw King Furlow, he was coming undone. It was the middle of the night and his son was dying before him, his daughter in hysterics at his side. Now he stands straight at a window that overlooks the workers in the distance. His pudgy frame has thinned somewhat, and when he turns to us, his eyes are tired, the skin purpled beneath them.

Near the window there is a large wooden desk, its surface free of any papers, I suspect because he has nothing to read through or to sign. No one is seeking his approval. He has lost control of his kingdom.

He waves dismissively to the patrolman, who remains out in the hallway and closes the door behind us.

"Ms. Stockhour, Mr. Cowl," King Furlow says with forced spirit. "I am glad you've returned."

Like the rest of Internment, I was raised to show respect to my king. Even after Alice's baby was taken from her womb at his command. Even after Lex went to the edge and condemned us all to the king's scrutiny.

But I am so very tired of it all. The false cheer. The curtsies. The polite nods. Pretending I should admire this cracked hollow shell of a king. And yet he seems to expect it, staring at us the way he does.

"Are you?" I say.

Basil tenses beside me. He could bow. I wouldn't blame him for it. He is, after all, the one who wants to play it safe. He wants us to survive whatever awaits us. I can feel how frightened he is by my candor.

But he doesn't bow to the king who ordered my death and the death of my family. And I must keep myself from smiling.

King Furlow's troubled face does not register a reaction to our small insubordination. He says, "When King Ingram said he would be returning two of my citizens, I couldn't be sure what his word was worth. I didn't know that he would allow you to come, and alive at that. I suppose it was too much to hope that my son would be returned. He did arrive on the ground in one piece?"

"The prince is well," Basil says. "He saw us off."

"Good, good," King Furlow says. "Please be seated. What is that you're holding?"

"Scripts," I say as Basil and I sit in the cushioned chairs opposite the king's desk.

No sooner do we sit, than the ground rumbles under our feet. The legs of the desk rattle against the stone floor. Basil and I start, but the king is unfazed.

"That would be the engine as the jet takes off. Ingram did say he would be taking it back as soon as he returned you two."

I have lived on this floating city my entire life with no way out, and yet for the first time I feel panic at the idea that my ride has left without me. My brother and Alice and Pen are off in a place where I cannot reach them. Sweat is pooling in my palms, and I clench my fingers into fists.

"Now then," King Furlow says. He paces the length of his desk before sitting in the chair behind it. He gestures to the papers Basil and I hold. "You say those are scripts?" The king seems to have gotten comfortable in his chair, but Basil and I are rigid, like two tightly wound toys ready to go off in motion once the string is released. "I shouldn't be surprised. I suppose King Ingram has sent you back here to convince the people of our city that they should do as he commands."

"Yes," I say.

"We find ourselves in a jam, don't we?" the king says. "It would seem that the sunstone in our soil contains a substance those on the ground refer to as 'phosane,' and King Ingram would like to use it for his own purposes. And my daughter, too trusting as she is, told King Ingram about our sunstone, hoping for an alliance between our two kingdoms.

"King Ingram has men camped throughout the city. I do not know how much he plans to drain our resources. But we are a small kingdom. My daughter tells me that our entire city is hardly bigger than King Ingram's castle. If we don't cooperate, what's to stop them from destroying us entirely, killing us all, and taking our dirt as they see fit?"

He's looking at Basil and me, and after a long silence I realize he means for us to answer the question.

Basil looks at me. I am the one who witnessed the bombs at the harbor. I am the one who knew about the phosane. I am the one who met with King Ingram when Princess Celeste was present. I am also the one who knows the most about Pen's theory about Internment sinking and something needing to be done.

But I am also thinking of what Prince Azure said, about my talking to his sister. He didn't seem to trust his own father, and I certainly don't either, so I must limit the information I give him.

"I do not believe that King Ingram will destroy us," I

say. "Not right away, at least. Down on the ground he's having trouble utilizing the phosane. He doesn't know how to refine it. I suspect he's ruining it in the process, which may be why he's taking as much of it as he can fit into the jet and then coming back for more." I swallow hard, steady myself. It is very taxing just to be in the presence of this king, trying to be civil after all he has cost me. "Havalais has bombs. They could destroy Internment in an instant. But—they are at war with their own neighboring kingdom, Dastor. The people of Havalais are tired and in mourning. They have lost faith in King Ingram, and I believe—I believe King Ingram means to use Internment as a way to regain their hope. If he destroys us, there will be chaos. His own people might overthrow him. It isn't like it is up here. There are thousands more citizens. There are thousands of places to run to. A riot could destroy the kingdom."

The king folds his hands on the desk. "How refreshing," he says, "to hear from a young lady who is not so idyllic as my daughter. You may have a head for politics."

I don't want a head for politics. I want my family back. I want to be at peace, whatever "peace" may mean now that so many things have happened that can't be undone.

"What I propose, Your Highness, is that we offer to be that symbol of hope for King Ingram. If his people love us and value us, he won't destroy us. And perhaps, rather than showing him how to refine our fuel, we could give it to him in small doses."

"You mean work for him," King Furlow says. "Slave labor."

"It's the only suggestion I've been able to come up with," I say.

The king looks at me for a long while with an unreadable expression, and then he looks to Basil.

"You must be tired," the king says. "Rest up now. This building is rather old, I'm afraid, and there's no running water. Someone will be in with water basins for you to get cleaned up." He claps his hands together and there's an eerie sparkle in his eyes as he adds, "There will be a party for your return. King Ingram's men will be present, so you would be wise to read up on his notes."

I would rather set my hair on fire than attend another party by now, but when the patrolman opens the door to escort us to our chambers, we follow. Though we are at the top of the clock tower, it doesn't feel much different from the dungeon, as far as design is concerned. The hallway is lit by small windows and candles that burn in sconces. It's a modest kingdom, nothing worthy of comparison to King Ingram's castle.

"You'll be staying here," the patrolman says, leading Basil and me to a small room that is modestly furnished. The stone floor is covered by a large woven rug, and the walls have been plastered and painted white. A single window overlooks the woods that surround the clock tower, and I can see the train tracks in the distance.

Above the bed, a small, framed picture hangs on the wall, of a long-stemmed purple flower open in a ray of sunlight.

"The chamber pot is behind that screen in the corner, and there are clothes for you in the wardrobe. The seamstress will be by later to make any adjustments if they don't fit. In the meantime, do make yourselves comfortable."

He closes the door behind us, and I hear a lock sliding into place.

I spend the rest of the afternoon sitting on the window ledge, staring out. Basil paces and then eventually goes still. When I finally look away from the window, I find him propped up on the bed, asleep, with the stack of papers in his hand.

I don't believe he's gotten much sleep this past week. I have been so worried about what will become of Pen in my absence that I haven't paid Basil much attention. Not that he has complained. All patience and understanding, he has worried in silence as we prepared to return home.

Carefully, I sit on the bed and slide the papers from his hands, set them on the night table, and lie down beside him. I close my eyes and I listen to his soft measured breathing, and as my own exhaustion takes me over, I beg myself not to dream.

9

The seamstress comes sometime in the evening to adjust our clothes, but they are a perfect fit. Basil in pinstripes, me in a simple blue dress that laces up the back. It is the color of the sky on a clear day, and the roughness of the familiar sheep-shaving fabric tells me that I have grown too used to the satin linings and softer fabrics they make on the ground.

"Better the evil king you know, right?" I say to Basil when our seamstress has left.

"Morgan, that's treason," he whispers fiercely. "Be careful."

He's right. I hate it, but he's right. We're not safe to speak freely anywhere.

A patrolman arrives to take us to whatever horrible affair King Furlow has prepared for us, and Basil takes my arm. I find comfort in the strength of his hold, him ever sturdy at my side.

Our footsteps echo throughout the old stairwell, which smells faintly of mold. What a juxtaposition: two kings from two different nations, one living so modestly while the other is perched on a sparkling throne, each of them menacing in their way.

Basil and I walk in silence, afraid to speak before these guards.

When we reach the lobby, through the windows I can see that the sun has begun to melt at Internment's edge. I begin to think of Alice, coaxing my brother to take a break from his fretting and have some tea, maybe eat something. And Pen, in Thomas's charge, fighting for sobriety. And Judas, who kissed me once in the endless grass, who loses every girl he dares to care for.

Without them, and without a home to return to, Internment feels like another foreign city on that round planet below us. It isn't home anymore.

I wonder in silence about Celeste, who has yet to reveal herself to us. And her dying mother, whom Celeste flew to the ground to save. I wonder if either of them is still alive.

By the time we reach the bottom step, I can hear the people talking just outside the clock tower. I can smell—almost taste—the warm air. I hear songstresses still chirping; the insects hold no grudge about having their land torn up. Or maybe it's just that they don't have a choice.

When we step outside, the chatter stops. Glass lanterns hang on wires between tree branches, flickering and alight with flames. The crowd turns to watch us step out into the night air, and I recognize so many of their faces. People from my building, students from the academy. All of them watching us now with hope on their tired faces, as though we can save them with some great answer.

"There they are!" King Furlow cries, arms outstretched for us as he moves through the crowd. Panting from the effort, he stands beside us just outside the doorway. "Morgan Stockhour and Basil Cowl. The ones who have been to the ground."

The applause is nervous and contrived, conducted by the king's exuberant gesturing.

Around the perimeter of the crowd, I see patrolmen, and also soldiers in gray—King Ingram's men. As long as they're here, King Furlow will of course have to play along. So will Basil and I.

The party is a dull and dreary affair. King Furlow parades us about, forcing us to tell stories about the things we've seen on the ground—the mermaids, the elegors, the rain.

It's clear that this is just a political move King Furlow is playing with King Ingram's guards. Nothing of substance is being said, and the workers and students in the crowd all seem exhausted and afraid. Basil and I try to find his parents, but they aren't here.

An hour into the affair, King Furlow leaves us to mingle.

Basil and I hang back against the clock tower's outer wall, away from the crowd, to catch our breaths. One of the guards in gray grabs my arm, startling me.

"Ms. Stockhour," he says. Before he's even gotten the words out, Basil has stepped between us. The guard is unfazed. "Both of you, come with me," he says.

"Where are we going?" Basil says.

"There is someone who requested a private audience with you."

"Who is it?" I ask. Why would one of King Ingram's men be working for anyone on Internment?

But he doesn't answer, only starts walking behind the clock tower. Basil and I exchange glances, and then I make the decision to go ahead. Whatever it is, it can't be worse than this party and what King Furlow has planned for us next.

We're led through a small garden, and then the plum court, which I recognize from the night Pen and I escaped our makeshift dungeon prison.

I hear something rustling in the shrubs that frame the perimeter of the court, and then a voice says, "Morgan?" and my heart skips a beat. There at a distance, hidden up to her shoulders by greenery, is Princess Celeste.

I'm too stunned to speak for a moment, and then all I can get out is, "You're alive." She looks well. Unharmed. And she's smiling.

"I knew you'd return," she says. She nods to the guard in gray. "Thank you, Curtis." She looks back to me. "He's a friend of Nim's. A lot of the guards are. From what I hear, there's a lot of unrest on the ground."

I walk over to her, all the while battling a suspicion that something isn't right. Why is she hiding here? Why hasn't her father mentioned her, much less forced her to make an appearance at his party?

She stays on her own side of the shrub. "Things on the ground are a mess," I say quietly. "King Ingram has no idea how to use the phosane, and the people are upset. The king has set up a factory, and all it's good for are the fumes."

"What about the Pipers?" she says. "Nim?"

"They're doing fine," I say. "And Nim sent this along to give to you." I reach into my dress for the folded envelope. I didn't want to leave it up in my room, where anyone could come in and find it.

I hand the envelope to Celeste, and she presses it between both hands, as though she can feel Nim's words throbbing like a pulse. "Thank you," she says, and her eyes begin to water. She dabs at them with her lacy sleeve. "It's been difficult spending all these months apart. He must be so worried about me. I know he must be wondering how I am, but my father has made it impossible for me to get word to him about what's happening up here."

"Is your father using you for some political strategy? Because there has been no word about you on the ground for months. The jet comes and goes with more soil, but none of us have known whether you've been alive or dead."

"My father is trying to protect me," Celeste says. "He has always treated me as a sort of . . . well, a pet. Azure is the one who will inherit the throne, and I'm just a spare of sorts. So when I returned from the ground with talk of uniting Internment with Havalais, he didn't want to take me seriously. I told him that King Ingram wasn't to be trusted, but that I had a plan. Nim and I had a plan to unite our kingdoms, in a way that couldn't be disputed or over-turned."

"A plan?" I say. "Nimble hasn't told us anything."

"I was rushed back home in such a hurry, we couldn't be sure that it would take. And it's too dangerous for me to send word with one of the guards. If the wrong person knows about it, I'll be killed and it will all be for nothing. All I can hope for now is that my brother will find a way to tell Nim for me. He deserves to know."

"I'm confused," I say. "What is this plan? What does Nim deserve to know?"

Celeste looks to the guard in gray, who does a sweeping glance of the perimeter. Then he nods at her.

Daintily, Celeste walks the length of the brush until she has found a clearing. She meets my eyes and for once she seems uncertain, nervous.

And then she steps out into the plum court, and I see her pregnant stomach.

My breath catches in my throat, and for an instant I think it's some sort of trick—a costume. But her worried stare as she gnaws on her lip tells me that this is quite real. I must sway a bit on my feet, because Basil puts his hand against my back to steady me.

"You and Nimble planned this?" I get out.

Her eyes brighten. "Don't you see? Whether it's a secret in his world or not, Nim is a prince. The king is his grand-father. And I'm a princess. Our child is going to be born of two worlds. The first ever! Just think of it."

"I . . ." There are so many questions, I scarcely know where to begin. "What does your betrothed have to say about all this?"

She waves her hand. "I told you, he doesn't care about me. My only worth to him is all for political gain. He came by to see me once, when I first returned, and I suspect my father arranged the entire thing for show, just so the kingdom would believe he was worried about me. But he doesn't know about this."

I'm trying not to stare. It's just that I've never seen anyone pregnant as young as she is. And out of the queue, at that. "But your father didn't arrange for you to have a termination procedure?" The words are sour on my tongue. That's what would have happened to anyone else.

"I have a good understanding of how these things go," Celeste says, seeming quite proud of herself. "I kept it a secret for as long as I could. Months. By the time he caught on, it was too late to do anything about it. Around the fourth month or so, there are too many risks. He was livid, of course, but he doesn't want me to be killed. Oh, Morgan, you look so pensive."

"I'm surprised," I amend. Though, really, should I be? This is exactly the sort of reckless plan she would come up with. I'm only shocked that Nim—cool, practical, level-headed Nim—would agree to it.

She reaches forward and grabs my hand. She's still holding Nim's envelope, and something about it seems to have energized her anew. "There will be more. You should go back to the party before anyone knows you're missing, but

I'll visit you as soon as I can—tonight if I can manage it. I'm so glad you're the one King Ingram sent back."

She's gone before I can think of anything else to say to her.

The guard in gray brings us back to the party. He leans between Basil and me. "There are those of us who are on your side," he says. And then he's gone.

10

I wish Pen were here. Undoubtedly she would say the wrong thing about Celeste's situation. The unkind thing. She would fill this silence with words, easily. That's just one of her many talents.

But she isn't here, and I'm left to face my own thoughts about it, and they frighten me. My anger frightens me.

The party is over and the door has been closed behind us. Basil lights the oil lamp and sits on the edge of the window and watches me.

I pace.

"Are you all right?" he says.

"Yes," I say. "No."

"Tell me," he says.

If Pen were here, she'd speak for me. I wouldn't have to say it. "I have no right to be angry," I confess. "It isn't my decision. Maybe she's got a coherent plan this time."

"But you are angry," Basil says.

I drop onto the edge of the bed. "Alice didn't get to keep her baby," I say, and I keep my voice low in case anyone might overhear. We've surely got guards keeping watch over us somewhere. "I saw what that did to her, and to Lex. It ruined their lives, and the king knew it would, but he didn't care. But Celeste can do as she pleases because she's a princess?"

My hands are shaking. I lock my fingers together and press them into my lap.

"Would you feel better if the king had forced her to terminate it?" Basil asks, and he knows me well enough to already know my answer. He just wants me to admit it.

"No, that isn't it. I just think it's unfair is all." I think back on what Celeste told me about the attraction camps, how scared she was that her brother might end up there if the king found out. I thought that being prince and princess didn't immunize them to our world's rules. But Celeste, cleverly and foolishly, slipped through somehow. Just this one time. I hate the unfairness of it, and I hate that, in spite of everything, it gives me hope. "I don't want her to terminate it," I say. "But I didn't want Alice to have to, either. And she's hardly the only one. My brother told me that there were lots of procedures when he was a medical student. Lots of people who didn't want to."

Basil is quiet for a long while, and then he gets up and he makes his way over to the bed. He sits beside me, stares down at my hands that are so tightly clinging to each other that my knuckles are white.

"Lots of people would find it unfair that she's having a baby out of queue," he says. "Some might be as angry as you are, but others might be less understanding. Don't you think there are even some out there who might want to terminate it themselves?"

I wince. I know he's right. "The whole point of the queue is to keep things fair," I say, repeating something I've heard countless times in class. "To abate jealousy. I do think there are people who would want to kill it—kill her if they had to. And with things being what they are, people are more likely to snap."

"Which is why the king is hiding her from the city," Basil says.

I nod. "The prince told me to find her when I returned home. Whatever her plan is, she needs my help. And I will help. For Internment, and to make sure she's safe. It's just . . . unfair."

"I know," Basil says. He puts his arm around me, and I lean against him. "Prince Azure knew what he was doing when he convinced King Ingram to send you back home. He knew you'd be just the one to help."

"What a foolish idea," I say. "Pen is the genius. Why me?"

"Pen is a logical thinker and a problem solver," he agrees. "But you've got a cooler head. You care about people."

"I've been told I'm diplomatic," I say, mockingly.

"You are," he says. "It's one of my favorite things about you. Don't undersell yourself. You're here to do something important."

"Oh yeah?" I look at him, and I'm startled by the

sincerity in his eyes. "And just what is that?"

He tucks a bit of stray hair behind my ear. "I don't know," he says. "We'll see." There's a bit of a grin tugging at the corner of his lips. He's worn this expression since we were children, whenever he had something kind to say to me.

"I don't understand you," I say, my voice nearly a whisper. "I cause you nothing but trouble, but still, you just— love me. Why?"

He tucks my hair back again, and this time he keeps his hand at my cheek. "Don't know," he says. "I'm out of my mind, I guess."

I lean closer. "Me too," I say, and I see his eyes close an instant before mine, and then I'm kissing him.

I can feel the rumble of the jet in my bones, and smell the fresh cut grass that spluttered from the blades on the ground, and I can hear the songstresses chirping outside the open window. He's everywhere and nowhere, his fingers moving down the length of my arm.

I forget about Princess Celeste and Prince Azure and the painfully desperate eyes of the people at that party. I forget about untrustworthy kings and spinning round planets, and I know that of all the places, and of all the people in this world and the one below, I am right where I'm meant to be.

Somehow, one of his hands has made it to my thigh, and I feel the fabric of my dress moving up and up as he knots the fabric in his fist.

"Basil?"

He kisses my jaw, and then right under my ear. "What?"

"I want to be honest with you." My dress has reached my hip and I roll my head back. He kisses my neck, and I wrap my arms around his neck to draw him nearer still. And suddenly I'm afraid to speak, afraid to ruin whatever has brought us to this moment. We have both lost so much and stand to lose so much more, but we still have each other, and maybe that's the only thing left that's certain.

"Honest about what?" He draws back just enough to look at my face. "Is this too much? Do you want to stop?"

"No," I say. "No, I want this. But you might not, after you know what I've done."

His hand is still on my thigh, and I'm sorry that I've said anything, that I may have put a halt to things. But no, he should know the truth. "I kissed Judas," I say. "Or—he kissed me, but I didn't stop it."

It's as though he has just absorbed a punch. His eyes are dark. "When?"

"Months ago, on the ground, right before the jet took off for the first time." My skin feels cold where he was kissing me.

"Do you love him?" Basil asks.

"No." I shake my head. "And he doesn't love me. That's not what it was."

He sits back, away from me. "What was it, then?"

"I don't know," I say. "It isn't about love on the ground. People our age just don't think that way. It's all about—about just being in the moment."

"Yes, I've been to the ground," he says. "I know that they all live without consequences down there. I've seen how that kingdom is run. But I assumed we were different."

"Better, you mean."

"Yes, better. I thought our way was better. I thought you agreed."

"We aren't better than anyone, Basil. Look at our king. He's no better than theirs."

"I'm not talking about kings," he says, and his voice is frighteningly low. He's never been so angry with me. "I'm talking about you and me."

"You asked me if I wanted to take off my ring," I remind him. "You said, 'You can call what we have a betrothal, or not, but I'll still be here.'"

I know he remembers. It was after the bombing at the harbor, and I'd just said I loved him as we walked past the charred remains of Nim's car at the fire altar.

"You said it," I tell him, desperate to wipe that look of pain from his face. "You said you'd still be here."

He stands and paces to the window. Maybe he'd walk away if he thought he could get out the door without being accosted by guards. "You didn't tell me for months. Part of you must have wanted him. Even if it was just one kiss, he's lived on in your mind, in secret, for all these months. You must have been replaying it over and over."

He knows me better than anyone else could. Better than even Judas could. And he's right. My knees are shaking. "You're right," I confess. "All my life I've known what to expect. Lex couldn't take it. He went too close to the edge, and even after I saw what happened to him, even after all that pain he suffered, I was jealous, because he did something brave. He broke an important rule that our world had laid out for him. Not a lot of people do that. I wanted to do that, and I was afraid. Even after we left Internment, I told Pen over and over that I was going to marry you, and I tried to keep her from drinking too much, and I was polite, and I was still living my life according to these rules."

My voice cracks. "And then Judas kissed me. That was the one thing I never expected to happen; I never saw myself kissing someone other than you. I didn't think I was capable of something like that. It surprised me that I was. And yes, I wanted it for myself. Not Judas, not even the kiss, but the bravery of it. "

"Well, I'm truly glad you got to experience your rebel moment," Basil says bitterly.

"I wanted to share it with you," I say. "Basil, please. I want you to understand."

"You can't share it with me," he cries, turning to face me. "That's the whole point!"

I look at my lap. Tears are blurring my vision. "I'm sorry." I shake my head. "I can't undo it."

"Would you even want to?" he asks.

After a long pause, I whisper, "No."

"Well, at least you're still being honest."

He turns back to face the window, and the silence between us is so painful, I can't stand it. I know that he's right to be angry, but I can't undo that kiss with Judas. I can't even bring myself to regret it.

I stare at the door and I contemplate using it. I know I

can't go far. But maybe I could just sit on the other side of it, put some distance between us.

Ultimately I'm not brave enough to move. I only sit on the edge of the bed, tears blurring my view of the floor, as the silence goes on.

I don't know how long it is before a soft knock at the door jars me from my thoughts. "Morgan?" Celeste whispers. The door creaks open and she peers into the room. "Oh, I'm so glad you're still awake. I saw the light under the door."

She has no idea what sort of tension she's walking into. Basil doesn't move from the window as she comes in and sits on the bed. She sinks back against her arms with a groan. "I've never realized what a chore all these stairs are, all my life running up and down them. Some of the newer buildings have lifts, but Papa refuses to install one here. He says it will ruin the structural integrity or some such."

She's barefoot, and with a glance I can see how purpled and swollen her feet are.

"Where do you sleep?" I ask.

"Our apartment is up one more flight, on the top floor," she says. "It's quite nice, actually. Mother has been too ill to leave for a year now, but she's got everything she needs up there. I've hardly been able to come down myself. I can't tell you what an ordeal it was coming back up after I met you in the plum court." She waves her hand over her head. "But I didn't come here to complain." She grabs my hands. "You've seen my brother, yes? How is he?"

"Travel agrees with him," I say.

"He wasn't happy about being made to go to the ground," Celeste says. "He's convinced that being down there so long has caused me to go mad. But as I'm sure you gathered, King Ingram forced my father's hand. He needs a prisoner. That's how he works."

"Isn't your father worried about your brother?" I say.

"Well—yes," Celeste says. "But the way he sees it, Azure is next in line to be king. And it's a king's duty to protect his kingdom. He should be willing to put himself in a bit of peril if that's what Internment needs." She squeezes my hand. "But Az and I aren't planning to do things our father's way. We've got a plan that we know he'd never go for."

"The baby, you mean," I say.

She pats her stomach. "The baby is more of a long term plan. It'll be born of two worlds and inherit both thrones, but not anytime soon. No. In the short term, before he left, my brother and I spoke with several of the guards and patrolmen. We learned which ones were to be trusted. We've been gathering intelligence about King Ingram and the ground. In fact, that letter from Nimble was stuffed with information about King Ingram's failed attempts to refine the phosane."

"I thought it would be all love letters," I say.

"Well, yes." She grins. "There was a bit of that, too. But that's neither here nor there." She turns her head to Basil, who has been listening in silence. "This isn't all girl talk, you know. Come over and join us."

Without a word he pulls up the footstool and sits across from us. He doesn't meet my eyes.

"You've come at just the right time," Celeste tells us. "As much as I can trust a few of the patrolmen and guards, I can't exactly go broadcasting my condition to the city. When my condition became . . . well, more obvious, my brother began doing all the speaking with the engineers. But in his absence, it'll be your turn."

"You want Basil and me to speak to engineers?" I say.

"Yes. Well, one engineer. He's head honcho over at the glasslands and you'll want to update him about what's going on with the ground. My father will send you there on some frivolous pretense of giving them a morale boost. He doesn't expect you to accomplish anything—it's all so the guards will have something positive to report back to King Ingram. But really, I've already arranged for you to speak to the head engineer. He'll tell you his plans, and then you'll report back to me." She bounces in her seat, and I wish I had the optimism to mimic her enthusiasm. "It's all very covert."

There's a sick feeling in my stomach, and I know the answer even before I ask. "Who is the head engineer?" There are several engineers, but there's one in particular who seems to be in charge of things, and whom I know to be brilliant, the way that his daughter is brilliant.

"That's the best part," Celeste says. "You've been acquainted. The head engineer is Nolan Atmus—Pen's father. He's a genius, of course. Several years ago he played a key role in the refining system that Internment uses to this day. He found a way to mine our soil more efficiently, so that we no longer need steam power. I can see now where that girl gets her brains, but I wish some of his diplomacy had rubbed off on her."

"Diplomacy," I echo hollowly.

Basil catches my grim tone, even if Celeste doesn't, and he raises a brow at me but says nothing.

"Listen to me going on," Celeste says. "I swear I haven't been this chatty all these months. Things up here have been looking rather grim." She smiles, and I can see how worn she truly is. "It's so good to have you back." She gives me a hug before she leaves. "Get some sleep. Tomorrow will be a big day."

The door closes, and I can hear her shuffling up the steps. Every little sound carries within all these stone walls.

Basil is watching me. I told him about Judas, the secret that's been nagging at me for months. But I won't tell him about Pen's father and the monster he truly is; that secret is not mine to tell.

"I'm going to sleep" is all I say. I move to the changing screen and change into the nightgown that's been laid out for me. I leave the dress rumpled on the floor, and without another word I climb into bed and close my eyes.

It's a long while before I feel the weight of Basil getting into the bed beside me. He turns off the oil lamp.

We maintain our distance, and eventually, somehow, I'm able to fall asleep.

11

All morning, I think about Alice. I've known her since the day I was born, and she has been in love with my brother all that time. Miraculously. He isn't an easy person to love, and I know that. I've seen the way that they argue, and it's always his fault, but it always gets fixed.

I've never fought with Basil. We have, despite our flaws, found it easy to love each other.

Until now.

I don't know how to fix this. I need Alice to tell me what to do when one of us has broken something this important.

Basil and I don't speak. Celeste is the one to bring us a tray of breakfast—fresh fruits and bread—and she is all chatter about the day's plans. She can't wait for us to speak to Nolan Atmus, the head engineer over at the glasslands. Maybe we'll even get a tour, she says. "That's a rare privilege," she says. "My brother and I have seen it, of course, but for a normal citizen it's a high honor. You're so lucky!"

Pen has seen the inside of the glasslands, but I don't say that.

Celeste slips a stack of folded papers into my hand. "Keep these hidden. Do you understand? They're for Nolan Atmus's eyes only. Top secret information from Nim."

I tuck the papers into my dress pocket.

After breakfast, a patrolman comes to our room to take us to the glasslands at King Furlow's request, just as Celeste predicted. He stops Basil in the doorway. "The invitation has been extended only to Ms. Stockhour."

"I'm sure my invitation was implied," Basil says with uncharacteristic boldness. "We go everywhere together."

"King Furlow has requested a private audience with you," the patrolman says. "Someone will be along to escort you shortly."

Basil and I exchange glances. He seems worried. "It'll be fine," I tell him. It's the first thing spoken between us in hours, and my voice sounds strange.

He nods.

There are two more patrolmen and a guard in gray waiting for me when I step outside the clock tower. I suppose they think I'll run away, but it isn't as though I have many options. Maybe they think I'll fling myself over the edge and hope for death.

Or maybe they aren't worried about what I'll do, but rather what someone might mean to do to me.

I'm led to a shuttle, which is empty aside from the guards

and me. We drive over grass, away from the train tracks, and through the windows I can see that the city itself has changed. There aren't many people, and the shops appear to be closed. I wonder if children are in class, or if they've all been forced to mine for sunstone as well.

The glasslands appear in the distance, and the shuttle slows to a stop.

"Up," one of the patrolmen tells me. I recognize him. After the fire at the flower shop, he was assigned to my building. I remember him holding open the door for Pen and me, telling us to be safe.

But if he recognizes me, he gives no sign. And without Celeste here, I don't know whether he's one of the patrolmen to be trusted.

I've never been this close to the glasslands before. I can see the beveled edges of the panes of glass, see the bolts holding the panels in place. The fence that surrounds the area is buzzing like a swarm of bramble flies, making my skin prickle.

Surrounded by a cloud of guards, I approach a gate where patrolmen seem to be waiting for us. "Ms. Stockhour?" one of them asks me.

I nod.

"Come with me," the patrolman says. And to the others, "None of you are permitted. You may wait for her here if you wish. This is the only entrance or exit, so there's no need to worry about an escape."

Escape? I could laugh. Where would I go? I suppose I could be like Judas and roam the wilderness for a few days, never staying in one place long enough to get caught. Only, this time there's no metal bird waiting for me underground.

The guard in gray tries to protest. He wants to see what's on the other side of this fence. But if there's one thing that makes the people of Internment bold, it's protecting our fuel source. Otherwise, what's to stop King Ingram from stripping us of our resources and blowing us right out of the sky?

I'm led inside by the patrolman from the gate. Once we have put some distance between ourselves and the others, he says in a low voice, "What is it like? On the ground? I've heard that there are thousands of kingdoms and that they shoot at each other for fun."

"You're not too far off," I say. Now that I've seen the ground, I'm no longer awestruck by the thought of it. Sometimes I even wish I could go back in time to before I left Internment. But then I remember that the king murdered my mother and quite possibly my father as well, and that I didn't have a choice.

"Are they barbarians down there?" the patrolman asks.

"People are people, regardless of where they are," I say. It isn't a yes or a no, because I don't have the answer. I used to think I did. I used to think that by living in the sky I had evaded some vengeful god's curse. I used to think that the ground was mysterious and intriguing. But as it stands, I've lost any sense of enchantment for either place.

"Mr. Atmus has been looking forward to meeting with you," the patrolman says. And again he lowers his voice. "He's going to help you."

"Is he?" I say. I hope my face doesn't betray the nausea I'm starting to feel, not only at the thought of facing Pen's father, but as a result of all the constant humming in this place. And there's so much heat. This place is meant to absorb the sunlight, and I suppose it stands to reason that it absorbs a lot of heat as well.

And despite everything, I am in awe of what I see. It's as though we are walking in a giant gemstone, or a betrothal band.

I see a few men and women working in the distance, taking notes, fiddling with knobs and steering wheels that are built right into the glass. Sun engineers. Internment's elite, the ones who give us the fuel for our trains and our lights.

When we've reached what looks to be the center of the glasslands, I see a small building made of brick, scarcely bigger than a water room, with a door but no windows. There's a glowing red lightbulb, and a sign that cautions people not to enter while the red light is on.

The patrolman steps forward and knocks on the door. "Sir?" he says. "You told me to inform you when Ms. Stockhour was here."

There's a long pause, and I hear shuffling within the building, the clink of something metal. And then the door swings open.

Pen's father stands in the doorway, wearing a denim jumpsuit, just like many of the other sun engineers. He looks from the patrolman to me with a distracted, almost deranged, stare that I know all too well. I hate how much he reminds me of Pen. She's even got his smile.

"Morgan!" he says, and makes room for me. "I've been waiting for you. Come in, come in." And then, to the patrolman, "Wait outside. See that no one disturbs us."

I will myself not to tremble. Whether the feeling is from hatred or fear, I can't tell. I don't want to be alone with him. I don't trust him, but more important, I don't trust myself. I'd like to take that pencil that's tucked behind his ear and stab him in the jugular.

But it's because of Pen that I don't. If I killed her father, I would be arrested, probably executed, and what good would that do her? And besides, we made a promise to keep ourselves safe and alive so that we'll see each other again.

I force a smile and follow him into the brick building. The door closes behind us, but despite being windowless, this tiny room is filled with lights. There's a wall made up entirely of glowing buttons in a gradient of colors. On an adjacent wall there's a small, flickering screen that shows a gray, aerial image of the glasslands.

"Sit, sit," he says, gesturing to two wooden stools beside the wall of buttons, next to a desk littered with papers, maps, and pencils. "I know it isn't very much to look at. It certainly isn't as spectacular as the rest of the glasslands. But it's the only place on Internment where I feel confident no one will hear us."

That hardly puts me at ease. Is this the place where he lured Pen when she was a child? Is this where it all started?

I fold my arms across my stomach and I wish desperately that Basil were here. Suddenly the air feels very warm.

"First things first." He runs his hand through his blond hair. "How is Margaret? Her mother and I have been beside ourselves all these months. When I heard that the king of the ground was sending someone back home, I had hoped she would be in the group."

He is the only one to call Pen by the name she was born with. Margaret. She's always hated that name with a vitriol I never understood until now.

"She's doing well," I say.

"Is she truly?" he says. "I know that she can be sort of . . ." He trails off. "I know that she takes after her mother, in some regards."

"The ground has suited her," I say.

I see a bit of her in his smile, and I force myself to look at the papers on the table instead. "What are all these?" I ask.

"Boring paperwork, I'm afraid. We gather daily reports from all posts to ensure that things are running smoothly. King Furlow is very particular about this place. Without electricity, the whole city would fall into chaos. Although I suppose an argument could be made that it's in sort of a chaotic state right now."

He leans forward on his knees, closer to me.

"What I really need from you is information about the ground. The princess said that you would be coming back with something for me."

"I suppose she means this," I say, and hand him the stack of papers from my dress pocket.

He unfolds the top page and reads it, and his eyes

brighten. "It's as I thought," he says. "That king down there on the ground hasn't got a clue what to do with our sunstone. His people are about ready to overthrow him."

"That's what I gather," I say. "So what are you planning to do?"

"Oh, let it happen, of course. We hardly need to concern ourselves with that greedy world down there. No, when it comes to the ground, we just wait for King Ingram to be assassinated. Believe me, it will happen. He thinks that he's holding Prince Azure as his hostage, but I guarantee that the prince has got a plan up his sleeve. I spoke to him myself before he left."

"But those notes are from Nimble Piper. He's the son of one of King Ingram's advisers." He's also King Ingram's grandson, but I don't say that, as I'm not sure whether Celeste has shared this with anyone up here. "You're telling me Nimble is part of a plan to assassinate his own king?"

Nolan Atmus slaps the papers against his knee in triumph. "That's what I'm saying. You seem surprised."

"I suppose it does make sense," I say. Murder hardly seems like something Nim would go for; he's so peaceful by nature. But then I think of the lost look in his eyes in the weeks following the bombing, after he'd buried his only brother and burned an offering to save Birdie. Maybe he's still trying to save her, and his other sisters too, from a king who would hurt them a thousand times over for his own gain.

"If that's Nimble's plan, I'm okay with it," I say. "He knows what he's doing."

"That's what the princess said as well. She seems to have a lot of faith in his politics. Splendid. Now we can discuss what to do while we're up here in the sky."

I can smell whatever redolence he's wearing. I smelled it every time I was in Pen's apartment. He has been everywhere all her life, and somehow I never noticed. He was always polite to me, pleasant. Much like the way he is now. How did I never see him for what he really is?

"For now," he says, "you should go along with King Furlow's plans. I suspect he'll parade you around for a bit. Let King Furlow's men have the illusion that you are trying to convince all of them down on the ground to aid his dying little kingdom. Let him watch your every move and believe you're under his thumb."

"That's it?" I say. "Just wait?"

"Just wait," he says. "I suspect King Ingram will be dead by the end of the month."

I walk back to the shuttle in a daze. I knew that Nimble would have some plan brewing, but murdering his own grandfather? Now I see why he was so adamant about my delivering that envelope to Celeste directly.

The shuttle begins to move.

I wonder how he'll do it. Will he stage an accident? Will he march up to the palace and cut the king's throat?

I wonder if Birdie knows. I think, after everything, she would want to help. It took weeks for her to emerge from her coma, and even longer for her to regain awareness of her surroundings. When she learned that Riles was gone,

I worried that the news would destroy her. She cried for days. She said that she hated the king, and her father too. Nim tried to quiet her, but only because he didn't want anyone to overhear her spouting treason.

I understand. My king killed someone that I love, too. I wouldn't object to someone killing him either. Maybe that's a good plan. Kill both kings and just start over.

The shuttle comes to a stop. I'm led back into the clock tower, smiling at the thought of King Ingram and King Furlow both dead. Justice.

I feel guilty for this thought when I see Celeste. Vile or not, King Furlow is still her father, and I know that she loves him, in her way.

She closes my bedroom door behind her, and her eyes are bright. "So?" she says. "Did you meet with Nolan Atmus?"

"Yes," I say. "He told me we're waiting to hear about King Ingram."

Celeste sits on the edge of the bed beside me. "Oh good," she says. "We can't discuss it here. You understand. For your own safety, it's best we don't talk about it in great detail." She giggles giddily. "But it will all work out, won't it? And I was so happy to hear from Nim and know that he was willing to help. Our child is going to be an heir to two kingdoms one day. Just think of it."

"Your plan for King Ingram seems . . . drastic," I say. "But perhaps necessary."

"There are two kingdoms at stake," she says. "Desperate times." She puts her hand on mine. "Listen, Morgan.

You've seen how brutal things can get on the ground. All that land, all that greed. There are two kingdoms at war over a fuel source that we offer to people on Internment for free. Money talks down there. It's terrible. And I tried to reason with King Ingram; you know that I did. But the truth is that he has no regard for anyone's life, not even the people in his own kingdom. If we let him go on, he'll strip Internment of its resources and then do away with us all if it suits him."

"I know," I say. "I do know that. But—" I cut myself off and think better of what I was about to say.

But Celeste already knows. "You're going to say that my father is the same way."

"What I was going to say is that I imagine every king is that way."

She gives me a weak smile. "I don't blame you if you hate my father, and certainly you're smart not to trust him. I don't always trust him myself. It's hard knowing that my father would send Az off to one of those torturous attraction camps if he knew the truth. And he would have made me have a termination procedure if he'd known about this baby in time to stop it." She takes a deep breath, composing herself. "But he means to do right by his kingdom. He loves Internment. He doesn't pose a threat to the city."

Maybe not the whole city, but certainly to those he's killed.

"Morgan," she says. All the joy and lightheartedness have left her tone. "I know what my father did to your family. I'm not asking you to forgive him. I'm not asking you to trust him. But you've got me on your side, and I promise that no harm will come to you or Basil. You trust me, don't you?"

"Yes," I say, and it's the truth. I do trust her. But I don't believe she understands everything that her father is capable of, and I don't believe she can truly give me the protection she's promising.

"Good." She pats my knee. "Now all we do is wait for chaos to break out."

"How will we know?" I say. "Once it's happened. How will word get to us?"

"Before he left, Azure said he'd work with Nim." She grins, and leans close to me, her voice barely a whisper. "They're going to kill the king, and before anyone can know what's happened, they'll have the pilot fly my brother back to the sky."

"But what about the others?" I say, panic bubbling up in my stomach. "What about my brother and his wife? Pen? Judas and Amy?"

"I'm sure Az will try to bring them along."

"Try?" I say. "Try? You can't very well kill King Ingram and then leave them behind. They could be killed in retaliation to prove some sort of point. Or arrested, and who knows what. You don't know what could become of them!"

"Lower your voice," she hisses. "I know how my brother can come across sometimes, but he isn't completely without a heart. He will do all he can to protect them."

"What if he can't?" I stand and pace to the window and back, my heart thudding.

"Morgan, if it does come to that, I think you need to be honest. Your brother was a jumper, and he and his wife ultimately took part in a plan to betray the government and escape the city. Judas is a fugitive. Pen—well, she'd do anything to keep Internment safe. I may not know a lot about her, but I do know that."

She's right. "What's your point?" I say.

"Morgan, sit down. Be calm. Think about it. If they can't be saved, don't you think they would find a way to be at peace with it? Don't you think they would die for Internment?"

"That can't be part of your plan," I say. My mind is going into such a panic that my vision is clouding. "You can't just sacrifice them like that."

"I've already told you that my brother will do all he can to save them."

"You don't sound too certain."

"Nothing is ever certain."

"You don't sound certain enough."

She frowns. "It was the only way. I hope that you can see that. My brother is down there, too. And the father of my child. They're at risk as much as everyone you care about. I'm worried. Do you think I'm not worried? But worry doesn't help. We've got to think positively. Have some faith."

"Faith," I echo miserably. "What choice do I have now?"

"That's the spirit," she says, undeterred by my glare. Pen once accused me of having a delusional sense of optimism, but the princess has certainly surpassed me there.

"I have to return to my mother," she says. "It's almost time for her lunch, and if I'm not there when she wakes up, she'll worry." She stands, and puts her hands on my shoulders. "King Ingram promised he would help her, you know. He promised me that he would fly her down to that big bright hospital in Havalais and the doctors there would make her better. He lied about that, and now she may not have much time left. So you see, we've all lost something in this mess, haven't we?"

I don't know what to say to that, but she doesn't seem to require a response. She drops her hands from my shoulders, and she leaves me with that.

And all I'm left to do is hope.

Basil returns shortly after the arrival of our lunch cart. He seems troubled, but he won't tell me what happened during his meeting with the king. Instead, he wants to know what happened at the glasslands. In whispers, I tell him everything. The plan to let Havalais murder King Ingram, Prince Azure's intention of returning on the jet, the potential danger to everyone from Internment. "She had the audacity to tell me that Pen and my brother would be willing to die for the cause."

"Pen would be," Basil admits. "You know she'd do anything to protect Internment."

"You're not helping."

"I'm sorry," he says. "I agree with you. It's terrible. But, in a way, it's the only plan that's got a shot at working. If King Ingram is dead, maybe Internment will be safe."

"Safe may be asking for too much," I say. "We're never going to be safe. We probably never were safe, not even before all this. We only thought we were."

He stares distractedly at his plate.

"Are you going to tell me what you and King Furlow talked about?"

He shakes his head. "It was nothing important. More rambling about what's expected of us in the coming days. That's all."

"Basil, I don't think I can survive all of this if we're going to be mad at each other. I can't stand the thought of fighting with you."

"I don't want to fight, either," he says. "I just can't get the image out of my head. And don't tell me it didn't mean anything; clearly it did, or you would have told me sooner. But it happened. It's done."

"It's done," I agree. "He came by to say good-bye to me before I left, and I told him that you were a part of me. I told him that I couldn't betray you again. I suppose that may not be worth much to you now, but—"

"It's worth a lot," Basil says.

"I meant it."

"I know."

He stares at his plate, forces himself to eat one of the grapes. When he looks up again, he offers me a smile, and I know that he wants to let this be the end of it. But I also know that something has changed between us. I don't know what it means, but I know it can't be undone.

The rest of the afternoon is a blur. The king sends us out

to the field where our jet first landed. A patrolman tells us about the sunstone mining process, but his words are very rehearsed. The guards in gray are listening to everything we say.

It isn't until after dinner, when the sun has just set, that Basil and I are granted a few moments of reprieve. We walk a narrow dirt path in the garden behind the clock tower. There are guards and patrolmen along the way, but if I ignore them, it feels a bit like Basil and I are alone.

"You've been wearing that worried expression all day," I tell him. "Is it because of what we talked about?"

"No," he says, and in a show of devotion he takes my hand. "No, it has nothing to do with that."

"Well, are you going to tell me? I was never good at guessing games."

He hesitates. "If I don't, you'll find out soon enough. May as well hear it from me."

"Hear what?"

He stops our walking, and as I face him, he takes my other hand. "I've loved you my whole life," he says. "Even when we were children, before 'love' was the word I'd use to describe it. And you were always running over the boundary lines, wherever we were. If there was a line to the shuttle, you had to move ahead. If there was a butterfly, you had to run after it and see where it was flying. And as we got older, your boundaries broadened. I've always sensed your need to wander."

I don't know that this is appropriate talk with patrolmen in such proximity, but I don't try to stop him.

Somehow I know that what he's trying to say is big, and I want to hear it.

"You loved to explore," he says. "So I wanted that for you. It doesn't surprise me at all that you found a way to the ground." He squeezes my hands. "I love that about you; you have to know that. I've never wanted to be the thing that held you in place."

"Of course you haven't. Basil, what are you trying to say?"

"This morning, when I spoke to King Furlow, he told me that our return to Internment may or may not be permanent, but he emphasized how important it is for us to give our people hope. And the way he means to do that is to make examples of us. Show everyone that even though we went to the ground and came back, and even though all of this mining is going on, things can be normal. They can turn out happily."

I search his face. I can see sweat forming at his temples. "Turn out happily?" I say.

"In marriage," he says. "King Furlow wants us to get married."

My mouth is dry and I can't feel my heart beating. I am hollow. "When?" My voice feels far away.

"In another week, on the first of September. He wants to hold a big ceremony."

"But there's never a big ceremony for weddings," I say, though none of this feels real. When Alice and Lex were married, I think he gave her a bouquet of flowers, and we had a small party for them in our apartment, but weddings happen often enough, and it would be impractical to turn them into a big affair.

"He says I'll get to see my parents and Leland there," he says lamely.

I nod. "Good. That's—that's good."

He frowns. "Morgan, if you don't want to, maybe we can reason with him."

"No," I say, because we both know there is no reasoning with King Furlow, and I don't want Basil getting killed because of me. "No, I think we should do it."

"Really?"

"It isn't as though we weren't going to get married eventually anyway," I say practically. "It'll be a little sooner than we expected, is all."

He tries to smile, and I can see how frightened he is. Of the king. Of this new plan. Of everything.

"I'm only sorry Pen can't be there," I say. "When she finds out I got married without her, she's going to throw a fit of epic proportions." When I laugh, Basil laughs too, both of us trying to make light of this bizarre situation.

All around us, the stars are bright and still in their sky.

I don't allow myself to wonder what's happening on the ground below our floating city. I can't afford the pain.

12

Celeste is surprisingly sympathetic when I tell her about the wedding. She tells me that I can pick any of her long season dresses and the seamstress will alter it to fit me. She can't allow me into her family's private apartment upstairs, but she sends the seamstress down with armfuls of dresses for me to choose from. Celeste shoos Basil from the room and sends him down to the garden with a patrolman.

"This is girl stuff," she tells him. "It wouldn't interest you."

He gives me a worried look but I nod, and he allows the patrolman to lead him away.

I drop onto the stool by the bed, deflated.

"He really is a sweet boy," Celeste tells me. "You should see the mess that I'm betrothed to. He has an unusual nose, you know, and I didn't quite know how to describe it until we got to the ground and I saw all those birds up close. Wouldn't you know it, his nose is exactly like a beak."

Despite everything, I laugh. "Now you sound like Pen," I say. "She's always saying things like that about Thomas, even if none of them are true."

"Oh, believe me, it's true," Celeste says, and holds up a paisley pink dress that only a girl with her confidence could ever pull off. "Not that his nose is the real problem. It's who he is. He's truly one of the most awful people I've ever encountered. Cocky, self-serving, and the way he looks at me—like I'm a buffet. Just the thought of being married to him makes me shudder."

"What does your father say?"

"Papa adores him," Celeste says. "His mother and father are both doctors, very motivated. Apparently they were both at the top of their class as students. And Papa was so impressed with the pair of them that he selected them from dozens of other couples in the queue to birth my future husband. It was sealed before the boy was even conceived, and months before I was born."

She holds up a bright green dress the color of grass. "Here, try this one on." As I move to the changing screen, she goes on. "I guess it went to his head, knowing that his sole purpose in the world was to marry the princess of Internment. Maybe he would have grown up to be a decent person if he hadn't had his destiny sealed, but I doubt it. And anyway, who cares? I'm not going to marry him now."

"What's to stop your father from claiming the baby is your betrothed's?" I say.

"He won't do that," Celeste says. "I won't let him. He won't have his way, not about this. Oh! Come into the sunlight. That looks so pretty on you. But it clashes with your eyes. I'm sure I have something with more blue in this pile somewhere. . . ."

"Do you have anything white?" I say.

"Lots of white. And pure white, too. Not that cream or beige stuff everyone else wears."

"Birdie told me that people wear white when they get married on the ground," I say.

Celeste begins plucking choice dresses from her collection and making a separate pile. There are a dozen of them, at least. Some with fake feathers, others with fluffy petticoats, others simple with straight hems. "I think a ground wedding would be nice," Celeste says. "Nim says that when we get married, we won't have to go to a church. That's what's popular down there—churches. But he says we can get married in a garden if I like, or on the ferry."

"Celeste." I sit on the edge of the bed and stare at the fabric of all the dresses. "Be honest with me for a minute. Are we really going to make it back to the ground? Can you say that with any certainty?"

"Not with any certainty," Celeste says. "One can never promise that. There could be a fatal virus pandemic tomorrow. Internment could fall out of the sky. The sun could explode. Nothing is certain."

"Is it probable, then?"

She heaves a deep breath, lays her dress down, and looks at me. "Here is what I believe. You will marry Basil in a few days, and maybe it will be sooner than both of you expected, but you'll treat each other well, and you'll be happy. Nim will find a way to"—she lowers her voice to a whisper—"kill that awful king of his." She clears her throat. "And then he will find his way back to me. He'll supersede his father and take over as the new king of Havalais; believe me, nobody wants his father in charge. They blame him for all of King Ingram's bad decisions."

"What happens then?" I ask. I'm trying to make her see that it may not be as easy as she believes, but she's determined not to.

"Then this baby is born and we all live happily ever after. The end."

"What about your father?"

"He'll see that it's for the best, once this all plays out."

She truly believes what she's saying, or at least she's trying hard to believe it. What I see is a big mess that's going to end with all of us dead and Internment a big scorch mark in the sky.

"Try this dress," she says, and hands me a simple white gown with billowing lace sleeves. "I wore it only once, to some ribbon-cutting ceremony at a new hospital wing or some such."

A year ago I would have been over the moon—marrying my betrothed and wearing one of the princess's dresses. A white dress, at that. Usually they are worn only by members of the royal family. If all this were happening under normal circumstances, I would be happy. Basil would be happy, too.

Instead, both of us are fumbling around trying to make this work somehow.

I try on the dress and then I stand before the small mirror on the dressing table. Celeste stands beside me, her stomach so swollen, it's surreal. "I love this one," she says. "What do you think?"

"I'm frightened I'll dirty it," I say. "I've never worn white before."

"It's only for one afternoon," Celeste says. "Just gather the skirts if you go into any high grasses."

"It'll do," I say. "Thank you."

"'It'll do'?" She pinches my cheek. "Come on. You can give me something better than that."

I smile. My reflection in the mirror seems strange. I've never seen myself in all white before, and I don't know who this girl is, about to get married when she ought to be at the academy learning about why the god in the sky loves her so much. "Do you think Basil will like it?" I ask.

"If he doesn't, he's an idiot," Celeste says with confidence. "If you were wearing this, I'd marry you."

I stare at my collarbone, framed with lace. So much like a woman, my mother told me several months back, before all this. She knew then what I didn't know. She knew all about the metal bird hiding in the soil below our feet, and she knew that something big was coming. I don't believe she asked for any of it. All she wanted was for her children to be safe, and to hang on to some semblance of the life she and my father had built for us.

But if she were alive, even with our world in ruins, she

would want to be here for this. She would want to see me get married.

Celeste frowns at my reflection. "You look as though you're about to cry," she says. "Oh, Morgan, don't. It won't be such a terrible thing. You're marrying someone you're truly in love with."

"It isn't that," I say. I take a deep breath, straighten my back, and steady myself. "If I have to be married at all, I'm glad it's to Basil. I was only thinking that I wish my family could be here." I look at Celeste. "I don't suppose you were able to find out what's become of my father."

She purses her lips together and then says, "I wish I had been able to find out. If Papa knows, he won't tell me. I did plead a case on your behalf. I told him all you had done for me, and that if he knew where your father was, and if your father were alive, to spare him. But that's all I was able to do. I'm sorry."

This news just gets absorbed into the existing numbness I've felt since my return. I nod.

"Here." Celeste pulls the stool up to the mirror and guides me to sit. "Let's work on hairstyles, shall we?"

In the week leading up to the wedding, the only time that Basil and I get alone is in the evening after dinner. The king has made a point to keep us busy, sending us to talk to the miners and the hospitals like we've done something that's made us famous.

The hospital is the worst of it. We're brought to see only the newborns, but the sterile smell is the same in every room.

When we at last step outside, I feel as though I can breathe again.

"Are you all right?" Basil asks me as we walk for the shuttle. My legs are trembling.

There are guards ahead of us and patrolmen behind us, and I keep my voice low, but I don't really care if they hear me anymore. "That place always makes me think of Lex. I hate it. I hate it, and I miss him, even though he infuriates me most of the time."

"He's okay," Basil reminds me. "He's with Alice, and he's infuriating her for the time being, until you get to see him again." He forces a smile, and for his sake I return it.

"Wherever he is now, I'm sure that's just what he's doing," I say.

"He's with the Pipers and Alice," Basil reassures me. "He's safe."

I know he's trying to console me, but I suddenly wish he would stop talking. His parents and brother are here in the city, and he'll see them at our wedding. I don't know if Lex or my father are truly safe. I don't know if I'll ever see them again.

We sit across from each other on the shuttle, and I'm filled with so much jealousy that I can only stare out the window. It's so strong that I'm certain he can sense it.

He reaches out and puts his hand over mine.

We ride back to the clock tower in silence.

The night before the wedding, I can't sleep. The clock tower strikes midnight and I can feel its chime rattling the walls. I stare at a patch of stone ceiling that's illuminated by starlight.

Basil stirs beside me. It's been nearly a week since our fight about Judas, and even though we've made amends, we haven't gotten very close to each other since then. I can still feel that argument hovering in the air around us, filled with the things we wish we hadn't said, and the things we wish we had.

"Can't sleep?" he says.

I shake my head against the pillow. "I'm thinking about the city lights in Havalais. If I looked out my bedroom window at night, I would see them in the distance, and sometimes I wouldn't be able to tell which lights were stars. It was strange at first, but after a while it was comforting to know that someone else was always awake, going about their business somewhere out there. But here there's just insects and stars."

He turns so that he's facing me. "Those lights are still on. We just can't see them."

After a long pause, he says, "When you think about Havalais, are you thinking about Judas, too?"

I turn my head to look at him.

"It's all right if you are. I'd rather the truth than have you try to spare my feelings."

"Yes, but not in the way you might think," I say. "I think about what it must be like for him to be living in a world Daphne wanted so badly to be a part of. I wonder if he's thinking about her, what those thoughts are. And I think that they'll always belong to each other, and how painful that must be, to have the other half of your destiny murdered."

In the starlight I can make out Basil's face, but not clearly. All I can really see are his dark eyes watching me as he listens.

"And then I think that if you had been murdered in that way, I would walk around every day feeling like I was half-dead. I would be just like him, in a way. I would look for you in other people, knowing the whole time I'd never find you. Or even anyone like you.

"He says otherwise, but that's why he kissed me. He was just looking for Daphne. And in a way, I was looking for you. I was thinking about you."

After a long silence he says, "If I ever lost you, I would be lost, too." He puts his hand on my cheek, and his thumb brushes over my lips.

My lips part, and I can taste his skin on the tip of my tongue. "It's you," I murmur. "It was always going to be you. I don't know how you could think it would be anyone else."

He moves forward and kisses me, and I feel at last as though he understands what happened in the field with Judas. Understands me.

"You never had to look elsewhere for me," he says. "I've always been here."

I close my eyes against the darkness. I don't want to think about what tomorrow will bring. I only want to know that he's here with me now, and that whatever we face, it will be together.

That much, the decision makers got right.

13

I have been told that more than a hundred people will attend my wedding. Honored specialists and patrolmen and even students from my academy. And Basil's family, of course.

I don't even know a hundred people. I can count on both hands the ones who ought to attend, and with the exception of Basil, none of them will be there.

It is strange to think that so many people will be in attendance for what should be a simple, ordinary affair.

Basil has been taken to a separate room somewhere to be fitted into his suit and dressed.

The seamstress has brought a standing mirror into my bedroom, and at Celeste's instruction she is pinning cloth flowers around the waist of my dress.

Once that's done, Celeste lights a fire in the fireplace and uses the flames to heat up an iron hair curler. She sits me on the stool before the mirror and sets about rolling curls.

"I saw that smile," Celeste says brightly. "Admit it. You're at least a little bit excited."

"I'm nervous, mostly," I say. "What is this going to accomplish?"

"Hope," Celeste says.

"Everyone keeps using that word."

"Well, it's all we've got for now," she says, twirling the curler so close to my scalp, I can feel the heat of it.

I stare at my reflection in the mirror. If Pen were here, maybe she would have some glib remark about what should happen on my wedding night. Or even some advice. She's the only one I'd want to talk to about it. But her first time was stolen from her; it was violent, and not what it was intended to be. I suppose that she felt changed by it, and I didn't notice. How could I not have noticed?

I feel a burn at the back of my head and I wince.

"Sorry," Celeste says. "It's my stupid stomach, getting in the way of everything."

"Does it hurt?" I ask.

"What—being pregnant? No, I wouldn't say that 'hurt' is the right word. But sometimes I feel like I'm in the body of a seventy-year-old. Once I sit down and get comfortable, it takes ages to stand back up again. My back aches, my knees. I never know what's going to give me heartburn anymore. And I can't get enough of the color blue."

"Blue?" I say.

"Yes. The other day, for example, I was looking for something to read in the library upstairs, and I came upon this old book with a bright blue cover. It didn't even have a title printed on it. It was just pure blue, and I wanted to take a bite right out of it."

"Colors don't have a taste," I say. "It would have tasted like paper, I should think."

"I didn't say it made sense."

"Did you?" I ask.

"Did I what?"

"Did you bite into it?"

"Please. I'm not quite that insane. Though I admit it's becoming a battle between what I know is logical and what I want. My mother says I've always been that way, though." There's a moment of melancholy at her mention of her mother; she wanted so desperately to save her, and now her chances are slimmer than ever. Even if the queen were to survive this ordeal and find a way to the ground, I don't think they would be able to cure her sun disease. Professor Leander died of that very thing.

Celeste slides the curler away from my hair, watching with satisfaction as the new curl bounces into place. "I so wish I could come. Papa told me I'm not even allowed to watch from the windows. He's got the entire kingdom thinking I've contracted some fever from the ground and that I'm all but dead. Meanwhile I'm trapped in this tower going out of my head, ready to start eating books."

She walks around me and begins curling the hair on the other side of my head. "Thank goodness you're back. I've been so bored and now it's like I have a living doll to play with. Before Azure left for the ground, his hair had grown longer. You may have noticed, it's almost to his shoulders. I asked if he'd let me style it for him and he about bit my head off."

"It's not that I mind letting you play with my hair, but how much longer am I going to be in the clock tower?" I say. "Basil and I get married and we just stay up here? We don't get an apartment? Do something other than be paraded around Internment?"

"You'll get an apartment," Celeste says. "A nice one with actual electricity, unlike this ancient place. It will just take a while. Once King Ingram is dead, I'd bet. Things will be better then."

With all this talk of dead kings, I wonder whether Celeste has ever admitted to herself, even once, that this kingdom would be better off if King Furlow were dead, too, and surely she's wise enough to know he'll never change his ways, but I don't think she's capable of admitting it.

She finishes with my hair and then sits on the edge of the bed, admiring me.

"You truly are lucky," she says. "I never believed betrothals were for the best until I met you and Pen and saw for myself that sometimes they are. Even your brother and his wife seem to get on rather well."

"Sometimes betrothals work," I say. "But sometimes not." I look at her reflection.

"It's not as though Az were going to get a fitting match, no matter what the decision makers decided," she says, and grins, but sadly. "You could line up the most beautiful girls in the city. You could even find a few who would put up with his ego. The heart wants what it wants, I guess."

I hope the prince is able to find what he wants, at least.

Celeste is pouting when the patrolmen come to take me to the courtyard. "It isn't fair that Morgan must be escorted by patrolmen to her own wedding."

"I don't mind," I say. Although that's not true. This isn't at all how I wanted my wedding to go.

"I'll be there for the ring ceremony," Celeste insists. "Papa won't be able to keep me away."

The stuffy heat of the stairwell smothers me, and as I follow the patrolmen down into the darkness that will end at the courtyard, Pen's words find me: *Our people would do anything to keep the city afloat.*

That was what she told Nim that night in the empty amusement park as the three of us lamented what we'd lost.

With each step down, I feel as though Internment is sinking below my feet, and I know that Pen is right. I don't know why this task has fallen to Basil and me, but we must do whatever it takes to save our city. Even if it means playing along with the king's silly plan.

I hear the music a moment before I step outside. The sun is high and blinding, the grass and flowers a perfect brightness that Havalais for all its wonder can't claim.

There's a trail of multicolored petals making a path to the garden. The trail ends at a field of poppies as red as a lake of blood. And there Basil stands in a black suit, a hard shadow against all the red.

He must surely be burning under this hot sun in such dark clothes, but if he is, he doesn't show it. This is the most elegant he has ever been. The brass music moves between us, the only breeze in the still air, and he turns his head just as I step onto the cobblestone clearing.

The corner of his mouth raises into a reassuring smile meant only for me.

People line the path between us. Old classmates from a lifetime ago. Citizens. People I've seen but seldom spoken to.

I don't have to look into the crowd to know that Basil's family isn't among them. I can see the sadness in his eyes, buried where only I could notice it glimmering like a fleck in a stone.

I approach him, and as I reach him, I glance up at the clock tower, wondering if I'll find Celeste spying from one of the windows. But all I see in the high windows is the cloudless sky reflected back.

The king himself is standing between us when I finally reach Basil, and he's holding a sheet of paper with the standard vows. He means to officiate this ceremony, then. Usually it's a patrolman. My father was the one to officiate Lex and Alice's wedding. I wanted him to officiate mine one day. It's just another thing that has been stolen from my family by King Furlow.

As he begins to read the words, the promises Basil and I must keep to each other, I imagine King Furlow lying dead in his own blood.

I don't hear the words that are being said. Basil takes my hands, and I know we're approaching the end of this thing, that a few words of consent uttered by each of us will make it official. And then while the others are celebrating, we'll be taken to the blood room and our rings will be filled.

"Morgan," King Furlow says. It's so bizarre to hear him speak my name so informally that I don't realize right away that it's my turn to speak.

I raise my head and look at him, cursedly alive and well. "Do you consent to these vows?" he asks.

"I . . ." Basil's expression is steely, unreadable. In a single word he'll belong to me.

And then the ground rattles under our feet, and there's a roar like thunder. The wind pushes all those heavy curls in front of my eyes, and I bat them away so that I can see what is happening.

Basil's grip on my hand tightens, and I'm not sure whether it's fear or hope that makes the laugh bubble up in my throat. There on the horizon is King Ingram's jet, tearing through the sky.

The alarm on King Furlow's face says that this arrival was not planned, and that the jet is not returning for its routine shipment of sunstone-rich soil.

The jet is also not landing in its usual spot, far in the outreaches on the other side of the fence. It's close to the city, too close.

"Come on," Basil says, and we run past the king and through the field of poppies. I lose one of my shoes as I go, and kick the second one away.

The king doesn't come after us. He has his own chaos to contend with. All his wedding guests are running away from the jet. Basil and I are the only ones running toward it.

14

"What about Celeste?" I yell over the roar of the wind. It smells like exhaust and fire and all the ever-advancing mechanical devices of the ground.

"She'll be safer where she is," Basil says.

I stop running, and, still tethered by my hand, he stops too. We're both breathing hard. I meet his eyes. "If this is an attack and they've come for King Furlow, we have to go back for her. Promise."

He nods.

The jet crash-lands at the fence that surrounds the city, causing it to collapse onto the tracks with a shrill whine and the sound of engines dying.

I double over to catch my breath, both of us choking on the fumes. There's a satchel abandoned on the ground. Everyone has fled in fear. They have perhaps grown accustomed to the jet's arrival at a safe distance, but something is clearly amiss this time.

The wind begins to settle, and after a long pause, the door to the jet swings open. "You nearly killed us!" Thomas yells. He is the first to stagger down the metal steps, with Pen holding the back of his shirt in her fist to steady him as they both stumble dizzily into the daylight.

"There are no scratches on any of you, so quit yapping. You all volunteered me to fly this thing in the first place," Nim says, following after them. The frame of his lenses is dented.

Basil and I run to them, and Pen sags gratefully against me. "Oh, thank goodness, a welcome committee that isn't wielding weapons."

"Give it a minute and there will be," Basil says. "What are you doing back here?"

"That's the problem with this city—its utter lack of communication." We all turn to see Prince Azure leaning in the doorway, not a hair out of place. "You haven't heard? The king of Havalais is dead."

Pen rolls her eyes as she looks from him to me. "He's been rehearsing that line for the entire flight."

"How'd I do?" the prince asks. He descends the steps as though they were flanked by adoring fans. He's looking at Basil and me. "Did our arrival interrupt a wedding?"

I ignore him. "Is King Ingram really dead?" I ask Pen.

"He is. It's a bloody mess down there." Her shoulders drop. "I tried to go back for your brother and Alice, but there wasn't time."

"They'll be all right," Nim assures us. "They're with my siblings someplace safe."

It's doubtful that Lex would have come along anyway, he's so insistent on never returning. Maybe it's just that he couldn't face what this city has become since we first left it. I couldn't blame him for that.

"I had hoped my father would be here to greet us," Prince Azure says, and I'm not sure whether he's serious.

"He is probably trying to quell the hysterical crowd," I say.

"Yes, well," Prince Azure says, and steps over the tracks and begins walking. "Shall we?"

The prince of Internment taking a casual stroll through the city is a rare sight, but if people are watching, they are doing so from the other side of windows, terrified of what fresh horrors this jet will bring with it.

"It was poison," Pen whispers to me as we all cross the tracks.

"Who did it?" Basil asks.

"I'm not sure," Pen says. "One of his own men, I suspect. So many have cause to hate him. All I know is that Nim saw it coming, and he woke us from our beds in the middle of the night and packed us into the jet. There wasn't time to get everyone." She gives me a reassuring smile. "Lex and Alice truly will be safe. Nim had to leave his siblings behind, too. This was less safe for them. And I did check on him every day since you left."

"How is he?"

"As stubborn as ever. Disgruntled—you know."

"I do."

"But he misses you. Truly."

I walk between Basil and Pen, and I'm so relieved to see her, I could almost forget the wars happening far below our feet and here on this floating city.

"We didn't really interrupt your wedding, did we?" she asks.

"You did, actually. But that's all right. I'd rather you were in attendance anyway." I catch her glancing at my ring. "We never had a chance to make it official."

"Good," she says, trying to sound as though she's taking this lightly. "Plenty of time for proper weddings after the dust has settled."

Being married is the least of my concerns, and I know Pen shares this sentiment, but the distraction takes us from the fear of what's to come. King Ingram is dead. That must mean that Jack Piper has assumed leadership. He isn't a better candidate. He's a man with horrors of his own to unleash.

The prince looks back at Basil and me. "Where is my sister?"

"In the clock tower, last I saw her," I say. "The king wouldn't let her outside."

"But you did see her? Talk to her? She's well?"

Nim also glances at me, and beneath his cool exterior I see someone who is tired and fearful himself. I hold his gaze for a moment before I look back to the prince. "Yes."

Thomas is trying to keep up with Pen, who won't look at him.

There's no smell of tonic, and she is alert and sober, which is all I need to know for now. "There's much to talk about," she whispers.

Prince Azure leads us back to the clock tower. Our wedding guests have either fled or are hiding in the offices behind closed doors. They have been trained to fear an ambush from King Ingram.

"Papa?" the prince calls. "Celeste?"

Silence. He opens the door to the stairwell and we follow him up.

"What has happened to this city?" Thomas breathes, horrified.

Pen shushes him, but the pain is all over her face. She loves this city more than our king ever could.

Azure calls out for his father and sister, and when we reach the door to the royal family's apartment, it swings open and Celeste is the only one there to greet us. "Az!" Her voice is a mix of fright and relief. She pulls him into her arms, trembling. "When the jet came, I thought it meant you might have been killed and King Ingram was coming to finish us all off."

"King Ingram is dead," he tells her, and in his gratitude to be reunited with her, he shows himself to still be human under all that pomp and conceit. "Where are Papa and Mother?"

"Mother is—she's been asleep through all this. She's gotten so much worse, Az. And Papa is off with his patrolmen trying to make sure everyone stays indoors."

She at last breaks their embrace and draws back to look at him. "I'm just so happy you're alive."

When she at last looks away from her brother and sees Nimble on the staircase behind him, it sends her into tears.

He is so weary and drained by whatever it is he's seen, and at last he has made it back to the girl he loves. "Leste," he says, and gratefully catches her when she crashes into him.

As they murmur quietly to each other, I hear her say, "I love you, I love you, I love you."

Pen jabs her elbow into my ribs. "When did that happen?"

I shush her.

"Oh." Celeste sniffles, wipes her wrists over her eyes. "I'm being rude. Where's my head? You are the first citizens to see the royal apartment. Ever, I think, isn't that right, Az?"

"It's never been allowed before."

"But we may as well allow it now."

"Clinging to the rules is pointless, given the state of things."

I forgot their bizarre ability to continue the other's sentences. What a set the pair of them are, with such similar mannerisms, the same blond hair and bright eyes.

Azure takes a deep breath, bracing himself before he says, "Mother?"

"In her room. She's refusing to let the nurse in anymore. She'll eat only if I beg her myself. Az, it's . . ." She fights off another sob and then she takes his hand and leads him down a dark and narrow corridor, calling back for us to have a seat and apologizing for having to step away.

I expected the royal family's apartment to possess some sort of luxury, but now I see that it's rather ordinary. Perhaps even smaller than my own was. Though the

sofa looks newly upholstered, its wooden frame is anti-
quated, probably handed down through the generations
of royals.

Now that Nimble has had time to find his bearings, he's
fascinated. He sits up straight in a wing chair upholstered
the same blue as the sky, and he cranes his neck to see out
the window.

"It's so . . . bright up here," he says. "The air tastes better. I didn't know air had a taste at all."

Pen sighs and falls back against the couch. "Yes, well,
enjoy it while it lasts. It'll all be ashes and a bit of folklore
for your city soon enough."

"King Ingram—my grandfather—is dead," Nim reminds
her. "I promised you I wouldn't let your city be destroyed,
and I won't let anyone else in Havalais be harmed over this
either."

"I don't see how you can promise that," Pen fires back.
"There is still the small matter of your father to deal with.
As I recall he's just as merciless, and next in line to the
throne."

Nim has nothing to say to this. He only stares down
the corridor where the prince and princess have disappeared. After a while he says, "I did speak with the oncol-
ogy specialist at the hospital. For your queen. But if what
she has truly is a cancer, it progresses in stages and by now
I don't know that there's anything we can do. Celeste tells
me she's been ill for more than a year, with no treatments
whatsoever."

Even Pen, who holds no sympathy for the prince and

princess, looks sorry for this. She knows what it's like to be powerless to help her own mother.

Just before the corridor, there's an old clock, and in our collective silence, each ticking is a small explosion. I try to drown it out, the sound of moments passing as we wait for King Furlow, and wait to learn what's to become of us.

When Celeste returns, she's alone and all traces of tears are gone from her eyes. She clears her throat and makes room for herself on the wing chair beside Nim. She doesn't explain her brother's absence, but presumably he's visiting with his mother. There is a faint medicinal smell to the air, which is stagnant and warm. Beads of sweat are glistening on Celeste's face, but somehow on her they look like cosmetics.

Nimble is watching her with fascination and caution, as though she may turn out to be a figment of his imagination.

She looks at him with resolution. "All right," she says. "Tell us what's happened."

"King Ingram was found dead in his drawing room. The troops weren't seeing results with the phosane, and after burying their loved ones following the harbor explosion, they were restless for revenge. I knew it was coming. I just didn't know when."

"So what Pen said is right, then," Basil says. "Your father is king."

"Not exactly," Nim says. "My father is dead."

Celeste lays her hand over his. "Oh, Nim," she says.

"It had to be done."

Pen leans forward. "You *planned* it?"

"It had to be done," he repeats, though there's a quaver to the words this time. "What you said was correct. My father was merciless. He served as the king's adviser. The bombings at the harbor were as much his fault as they were the king's." He looks at the floor, but then thinks better of it and raises his chin, meeting none of our eyes. "Birdie and I talked it through. We took no pleasure in it, but we agreed it had to be done."

"You're . . ." Celeste is watching him. "That makes you the king of Havalais."

"If you'd like."

"It's not 'if I'd like.' It's a fact. Your grandfather was the king, whether or not he cared to claim your father as his son. Your father was first in line; you were second."

"I don't know that patricide makes me worthy of the throne."

"Worthy?" Celeste asks. "The people of your kingdom will probably hoist you onto their shoulders and have a party in your honor." At his dead expression, she drops her shoulders. "Sorry, Nim."

"Whether or not I'm king, I'm the one who needs to speak with your father now about the state of things."

"Az and I will go with you," Celeste says. "We know how to talk to him. He can be unreasonable."

"Kings always are."

The city is silent beneath us. The window is open, letting in only the sound of air moving through trees.

It feels like ages pass before there's the sound of movement in the stairwell. Voices. Celeste straightens in her seat and listens. "Papa is back. He'll be going to his office. I'll get Az, and the three of us will go together."

She struggles to her feet, and Nim rises to help her. They steal a moment to look at each other. Only a moment. That's all they can afford right now.

My heart breaks for the pair of them. Beside me, Basil is frowning, and I know he's also wondering how this can possibly end well for us all.

An hour passes, and we sit in absolute silence, as though the walls themselves might reprimand us for daring to disrupt the royal air. The queen is bedridden down the hall, and I wonder if she knows we're here, or if she is too far gone to care either way.

Finally, Pen turns to me and says, "How long before it stops being inappropriate for me to ask what has happened to the princess?"

"It seems fairly obvious," Thomas says.

"It's her latest great idea," I say, too tired and anxious to be cynical. "She can't take all the credit, though. Nim went along with it—obviously. They wanted an alliance between their two worlds, and what's more solid than a new heir to two thrones?"

"It isn't all that stupid," Pen concedes. "They're both royalty. Still, with all the forced terminations in the city, there's bound to be some outrage."

"The king has kept her hidden away for months," I say. "The kingdom thinks she's ill. I fear what would happen if they knew the truth."

"I'm sure this will all go horribly wrong," Pen says, with forced cheer. "But it's a valiant effort, I'll give them that."

I put my hand over hers. I truly believed I might never see her again. There is much I want to say to her, but for now, Basil and I tell Pen and Thomas about the wedding they interrupted, and the time we've spent trapped in this tower, and the forced pleasantries in a city that knows something big is about to happen, and that Basil and I cannot possibly be the thing that saves it.

15

In a few minutes there will be a citywide broadcast to announce the death of King Ingram. So Celeste tells us, at least, as she frets and paces in the royal apartment.

"Isn't it a bit hasty to make that announcement?" Pen says, with no hostility for once.

"Yes," Celeste says. She's chewing on her knuckle. "But it gives our city the upper hand. My father's men have gathered all of King Ingram's men. They're being held in interrogation in the basement cells. Their loyalty to Havalais will be determined. Anyone who poses a threat will be executed. Harsh, I know, but I suspect that most of them will stand on our side. What other choice do they have?"

"We're on Internment," I say. "There's only one side to stand on. The other side is over the edge."

Her laugh is nervous and a bit hysterical.

"Sit down," I tell her. "There's no sense working yourself up while we wait."

"Wait," she spits back. "All I've done for months is wait. I'm so tired of it. Aren't you?" She shakes her head. "I can't leave this to my father, Morgan. He's the king, yes, and he's in charge of this city, but he's so . . . outdated."

"I would have opted for 'psychotic,'" Pen says.

"My mother is dying because of his fear of expanding our medical technology," Celeste goes on, ignoring her. "It isn't just medicine, though; it's all technology. This bloody clock tower doesn't even have electricity. Up until now we've had only so much room to grow on this patch of land, but now we have the entire ground. If we handle this properly, we can make Havalais into an ally, but Papa will make them into an enemy. He's scared of them and he's hateful, and he'll do the wrong thing, I just know it."

She walks for the door, and I reach her just as she's put her hand on the knob. "You can't go out there," I remind her. "Be reasonable. No one in this kingdom knows about the state you're in."

"Well, it's time that they do," she says. "Isn't hope our best ally? King Ingram is dead. What's more hopeful than a child who can bridge two worlds? What could be stronger than that?"

"Injustice," I say. I move between her and the door, and the knob is pressing into my back. I lower my voice. "You know a lot about this city, but its rules have never entirely applied to you."

"That's absurd. I—"

"Do you know what happens when people conceive children outside of the queue?"

"Of course I do," Celeste says. "They have a termination procedure. That rule would have applied to me, too, under the right circumstance. But—"

"There's never a right circumstance," I say. "Believe me. You may go out there bearing all the hope in the world. You may even have the means to solve all of the city's problems, appease all of its fears. But it won't matter. They'll hate you. They'll riot. That's the reason your father is keeping you out of sight. Don't you understand?"

Celeste is looking into my eyes, and I can see that she believes me. Much as she tries to be a diplomat, there will always be a divide between the kingdom's rulers and its citizens. We each represent a different view of the same world.

She's quiet for a moment, and then with renewed spirit she says, "Then you have to go." She nods over her shoulder at Basil. "Both of you. You have to force your way into the broadcast. The city loves you. Of course they do. You both represent the citizens better than my father or brother or I ever could. And Nim is an outsider; they'll be wary of him no matter what he says."

"I—" My voice catches. "And say what?"

"The truth. That you've been to Havalais. That the people there are not greedy like their king. Tell them it's a wonderful place, and that Havalais would make a strong ally, not an enemy. I don't have to tell you what to say. You're so good at seeing the best in people."

I look to Basil, who is walking toward me. "I think she's

right," he says. "We've lived in both worlds now. And you especially, after what you lived through at the harbor."

I hope I won't be made to speak about that. It still haunts me, and if I'd never left Internment and seen the ground for myself, the stories of bombs would scare me all the more. Havalais is recovering now, though its harbor will never be the same, but Internment would have been obliterated completely.

"All right," I say. "I'll see what I can do."

There isn't time for Basil or me to change, so Celeste runs her fingers through my windswept hair in an attempt to make me presentable, fits Basil's jacket onto his shoulders, and pushes us out the door.

"Wait!" Pen runs after us and meets us on the first step. She grabs my shoulders. "Tell them what I told you that night in the theme park."

"Do you really think that's wise? Now?"

"They need a bit of fear to keep them listening. They need to know that we'll help them."

She has been right about so many things before. I nod. "You should be doing this instead of me," I say.

"She doesn't have the social graces," Celeste says. "Hurry now."

Basil and I are left to make our way down the spiraling staircase, guided only by flickering sconces. "We'll be lucky if we aren't thrown in with the other prisoners for this," I say. "It's treason."

"Is it treason to intercept a king's broadcast if you're doing it under the order of the princess?" Basil says.

"Maybe 'treason' is the wrong word. There probably is no word for what we're doing, because it's that insane."

"All of this is," Basil says. "But you must agree that the princess made some good points."

"Yes, which adds to the madness. Celeste Furlow, the voice of reason."

We follow the directions Celeste gave us, through the lobby and down another stairwell belowground. The smell of mold and dust is overwhelming, but I hear the faint whine of something electrical. Light is flickering through the cracks in the door. There are voices on the other side.

The broadcast room. Normally there would be patrolmen guarding restricted areas, but with all the hostages from Havalais, the patrolmen have their hands full.

"Do we just barge in?" Basil says.

"No one's here to stop us," I say, and reach for the knob. King Furlow is standing in a sea of wires, looking flushed and fatigued. Behind him hangs a painted mural of Internment as seen from the outside. It was used for a festival some hundred years before, and it often serves as one of his backdrops.

He was in the middle of a sentence when we barged in, but now he has stopped to watch as we pace toward him and take a place at his side. There are three patrolmen—one of whom is operating the camera—and when they try to stop us, King Furlow waves them off. I was prepared for outrage, but he seems relieved that we're here to shoulder some of the burden. Nim and Prince Azure aren't with him.

"Citizens," he says, "you remember our bride- and

groom-to-be. Their own wedding was interrupted by the jet's arrival. So you see, this has hurt us all, but it's to a good end. My son, the prince, has brought word that King Ingram is dead."

"The wedding doesn't matter to us," Basil says. He casts a quick glance my way, as though he fears I might take offense, but if anything I'm relieved. He straightens his back and goes on. "The wedding was merely a distraction from Internment's hardship. But now King Ingram is dead, and you won't have to worry about more of our soil being taken. You can stop digging. Morgan and I have spent time on the ground. We've met its citizens. They never wanted to take so much from you; it was their king all along."

He's right, but I fear that no one will believe him. The people of Internment have been conditioned to fear the ground, and this nightmare has only fueled that fear, and even hatred. I gather my strength and say, "The ground is not very different from us at all. The city below us is beautiful. Its people were welcoming and kind. And they've been suffering too." I begin to describe the bombings at the harbor, going into such detail that the awful memory draws itself within my mind, brushstroke by brushstroke, revealing a coloring I never wanted to see again.

I stand bathed in the bright lights and I stare into the camera lens the whole time, never letting myself think that anyone is on the other side of it. I have no way of knowing if they'll agree with what I'm saying. Now that I've seen the ground, lived there, I hardly remember what it was like to be so uncertain.

"There's more," I go on. "Since the beginning of Havalais's efforts to mine our fuel, Internment has begun sinking in the sky. One theory is that the frequent arrival and departure of the jet is weakening the wind barrier that keeps us in place." I do my best to sound scientific, wishing all the while that Pen could be here to explain.

But a scientific explanation is not needed. The worry registers on King Furlow's face. "Sinking," he breathes. Then, "Cut the cameras."

The buzz of electricity dies away, and the king steps forward and turns to face us. "Is that true? Internment is sinking?"

"Yes," I say.

"How can you be sure?"

I hesitate. I do believe what Prince Azure said about Pen being in danger if the king were to know how truly valuable she could be to his cause. I have never been a good liar, but for Pen's sake, the lie slips out, "I was measuring it." I do my best to explain the sphere of wind that surrounds the city, and the threat that the jet's activity will pose to us over time. "I don't think it's too late," I say. "If the jet stops coming and going, Internment will stay put."

The king paces the length of the room, stepping over wires, pondering. "You," he says to one of the patrolmen standing by the door. "Escort these two back to their quarters while I mull this over."

"Are you sure you should have told him all of that?" Basil whispers once we're back in our room and we're alone. "What will he do with that information?"

"It was Pen's secret and she wanted it told," I say. "She must believe it will serve some purpose. She's never been wrong."

Basil frowns worriedly at the window, and I reach forward to put my hand over his.

We don't mention my father. The thought of him hangs heavily in the silence that falls between us, along with the many fears we don't confess.

16

Our meals are brought to us without a word. Night begins to fall, bringing with it the familiar trill of hopping songstresses.

Basil lights the candle in our lamp, and we talk in low voices, ever mindful about being overheard.

"I think he's dead," I say. I'm sitting on the window ledge, hugging my knees. I stare at my faded reflection in the glass. "My father. I think he's dead."

"Morgan—"

"The worst part will be the not knowing. The never knowing." I steal a glance at him. "He wanted Lex and me to leave this city. He and my mother wanted us to be someplace safe. I don't even know if such a place exists."

Basil has been sitting on the edge of the bed, and now he stands. "If you want to find out what happened to your father, now is the time to look for him. The patrolmen and the king and everyone else are busy dealing with the after-math of King Ingram's death."

I laugh bitterly. "Where would you propose I start?"

"The basement cells," he says. "That's where everyone's being kept, isn't it?"

"We'll be seen," I say. But I feel that cursed hope creeping up in me, putting an ache in my chest, and I know that I can't let this opportunity slip by now that it's been introduced to me. "Okay," I say. "Okay. I've been to the basement only once before, but it's like a labyrinth and there isn't electricity. We may be able to move in the shadows."

I know it's foolish to embark with any optimism. I see the state that Internment is in. From the moment the first explosion hit the harbor in Havalais, we have all been trapped in a dream of a world that is covered in old roots and dead vines. We dig for traces of our old lives. We think we hear our loved ones calling beneath the rubble, so we clear it away, hearts pounding, breathing quickly. But time and again we unearth nothing. Nothing but bits of sun-stone that go to waste.

The clock tower, like the night itself, is silent and still. I could almost believe that there was no life beyond Basil and me moving in the darkness. There isn't even the distant thrum of the train speeding by; there hasn't been for hours.

We reach the door that will lead us to the basement and I stop and take a steadying breath.

Basil is watching me. In the faint glow of a candle sconce that accents the wall, his eyes are round and dark. I don't need to ask the question that's plaguing me, because he already knows it, and I know his answer.

What if we don't find him?

We look elsewhere. We keep looking. That's all we can do.

I turn the knob; there's a staircase leading down. I swear this building is nothing but stairs and echoing walls. I can hear voices farther down, murmuring. Metal rustling—shackles? The prince and princess held Pen and me hostage using string, but it would surely take more than that to restrain a hundred men from Havalais.

I'm so fixated on the dim light at the bottom of the stairs, I don't notice the body coming up behind me until it's too late, and he's grabbed my arm. "Stop right there."

I don't struggle. Too easy to fall down these steps. He's got Basil, who also obliges but shoots him a venomous glare. The man prods us down the steps and I struggle to keep up. I should have foreseen this; of course I should have. I'm not frightened at all, only disheartened. My heart sinks like a stone in my chest.

Did I really believe I could walk down here and find my father among the prisoners? I was raised to believe that things could be so easy, so attainable. Everyone I ever loved lived within the confines of a train track. My world was laid out so neatly before me. How could I have wanted more? I didn't know the consequences of more.

"Your Highness! I've caught two break-ins trying to get downstairs. Where should I put them?"

We've reached the bottom of the stairs, and my shoulders drop with relief when I see Prince Azure standing before us. "Let them go, you bloody idiot. They're not break-ins. They're *guests*. Haven't you heard about the wedding that was interrupted by the jet?"

The man unhands us, and my arm throbs from the ghost of his grip.

"I'm sorry, Your Highness. I couldn't see them in the darkness."

"Don't apologize to me. Apologize to them."

He nods to me, then Basil, muttering his apologies, and it's strangely gratifying. After he's left, Prince Azure regards us. There are candle sconces lining the corridor of closed doors, and the light traces the sharp angles of his face. "What brings you down to my humble hovel?"

I hesitate, and Basil answers for me. "We were looking for a specific prisoner."

"Ah, yes," the prince says. "Let me guess. Your father, is that right? My sister told me all about that when she first returned, and for her sake I investigated. She feels truly indebted to you, Morgan. But, sadly, nothing came of the search. Your father isn't here, and if he's still alive and has any brains, he won't let himself be found."

If he's still alive.

I bury the enormity of those words. I cannot afford to open that pain anew.

"Best to focus on those we can help, yes?" Prince Azure says, and I do believe he is trying to console me, in his way. He claps a hand on Basil's shoulder and mine and steers us down the hallway. "You aren't allowed down here normally, but since you've found your way, there's something you should see."

All of the doors are guarded by patrolmen. There's talking going on behind some, and eerie silence behind others. "Internment has been in a state of madness for months, hasn't it? My father is quite overwhelmed. My mother doesn't have much time, let's be honest. And my sister is madder than usual."

"Hard to tell what's usual with her," I say.

The prince laughs. "Yes, I suppose. She was always a crazy thing. Maybe we both were. But then, that's the price of growing up in this place, with only each other and the spiders in the cracks to keep us company. And don't mistake my candor; she's a fool, but I will take her side always, even when she goes off and gets herself into predicaments like the one she's in."

I can't help feeling jealous. My brother and I care a great deal about each other, but he's never seemed to agree with a thing I've done, and I don't understand his decisions either.

"I don't know what to make of this boy she's dragged into our lives," the prince goes on. "Nimble Piper. I know only that he's important to her, which means I've been tasked with protecting him."

"Protecting him?" I say. "From the people of Internment?"

"The people of Internment don't know he exists, and besides they're no threat to anyone," the prince says. We've been walking down a long hallway that's been narrowing with each step. The stone floor has given way to raw earth, and the patrolmen stand guard in the glow of candles, several paces away from the only door in this primitive hall. Prince Azure raises a key to the lock and pushes the door open. "The thing I must protect him from is my father."

A candle flickers on the wall, nearly dead. Below that, slumped and beaten, is Nim.

17

My breath catches in my throat, and as I struggle for words, Basil says, "You can't treat him like this. He hasn't done anything!"

"My father is the king. He can do whatever he likes," the prince says. "It was stupid for this boy to come back here after what he and my sister did. Papa has spent these past months wanting to murder him. If I hadn't intervened, he might have."

I rush across the dirt floor and kneel at Nim's side. He's lying on his back with his wrists bound before him, his eyes bruised and swollen. When I touch his cheek, he sucks in a pained breath. It takes a moment for me to realize that the word he's trying to get out is "Celeste."

"No," I say. "It's Morgan. Can you hear me?"

He swallows hard. "Leste."

"She's all right. She's just upstairs." Though from where

he lays, upstairs might as well be a world away.

"I doubt he can hear you," Prince Azure says. "He's been muttering for hours." He closes the door behind us, entombing us all in this room with stale air rife with mold.

I look up at the prince standing over Nim's lifeless body. "We have to get him out of here."

"Believe me when I say that will make it worse. There's nowhere to go. The jet is under heavy guard, and where could we possibly hide him that he won't be found when my father realizes he's gone?"

"Then what's your plan?" Basil asks, venom in his tone. "Even if you can stop your father from laying a hand on him again, he'll die if he isn't cared for."

"I am—" The prince lowers his voice, kneels beside me. "I am caring for him. I've put salve on his wounds, and earlier I brought him some water, as much as I could sneak in."

I lift the hair from Nim's face and find a bloody gash that's been coated with a thin line of cream.

"Does Celeste know?"

"No," the prince says, "and she can't. In her condition, something like this would kill her."

"She isn't as fragile as all that," I say.

The prince laughs. "Fragile? No, she isn't fragile. But as I said before, she's a fool. She would hatch some half-baked rescue mission, be caught, *of course*, and be lynched by all those citizens with bleeding hearts about the queue. Even the king himself couldn't save her then." At my startled expression he says, "Oh yes, I'm well aware how much the people hate the termination procedures and the queue. There's much my father should change but is too stubborn to. He's the one they should lynch, but that won't matter. They'll trample my sister to death in a riot, and that's if they don't cut the bloody thing out of her first." He says this so simply, as though it's a science. "No, you and your husband-to-be are to go back up to your room, and when you see my sister, tell her that all is well and that Nimble Piper and our father are discussing strategies, or whatever it is she expected to happen."

"I can't just leave him," I say.

"If you want what's best for him, you will," the prince says. He and his sister both fancy themselves expert politicians, and from what I've seen they both make poor decisions with amazing ease, but still, just this once I believe he's right.

I lean close to Nim and say into his ear, "Hang on."

The prince escorts us back to the main level, and before he turns back into that awful basement, he says, "Look after my sister. She needs someone who will do that for her."

"I will," I say, and frown as he closes the door behind him. I turn to Basil, helpless.

"For what it's worth, I think he's right," Basil says. "We're in dire straits when one of the royal children is the voice of reason, aren't we?"

When we return to the darkness of our room, I climb under the covers and face the window. The moon is an eye that's suspended midblink. I cannot face Basil. I cannot face anyone. I keep seeing Nimble's wounded face, his bleeding mouth. Another Piper broken.

Birdie survived her wounds, I tell myself. Nimble will too.

After a long silence, I whisper, "Are you still awake?"

"Yes," Basil says.

"King Furlow has to die."

Celeste is in high spirits. Basil and Thomas have been whisked away by a patrolman to help motivate those assigned to clean the mess made by the jet so that the trains can resume soon. Celeste, Pen, and I spend the morning in the living room of Celeste's apartment, sharing bowls of strawberries and grapes. It isn't the arrival of the jet that has reinforced her optimism. It isn't the broadcast or the death of King Ingram. It's Nimble's presence.

"How did he seem when you talked to him? Was he worried? I bet he was worried. He's always so concerned about me; it's sweet, really." Mercifully, she doesn't wait for me to answer. "Hold that thought; I've got to use the water room."

After she's gone, Pen leans toward me and says in a low voice, "All right. Tell me what's really going on. I can read your face like a book. Is he dead?"

I glance down the hallway after Celeste. "Not yet," I whisper. "But it's bad. He's in one of the cells. If I didn't know better, I'd think an animal had attacked him."

Pen winces. "What's the plan to get him out of there?"

"The prince is going to keep him alive while his father figures out what to do next."

Pen sits back against the couch, fretting. "Do you think

the prince will truly keep him alive? I wouldn't trust him as far as I could spit."

"I wouldn't either," I say, "but I believe he will, for Celeste."

Celeste returns and drops unceremoniously beside me. She looks as though she's just been ill.

"Are you all right?" I say.

"Oh, yes, fine, just getting toward the end is all," she says. "Truthfully I'm glad the baby is going to be born here. Medicine on the ground is more advanced for sure, but if there's one thing our doctors do well up here, it's this." She gives a weak laugh. "But then, our population is such an issue, I suppose they have to regulate it the way they do."

Despite her upbeat tone, she doesn't look well. I put my hand on hers. "Maybe you should rest."

"How can I?" she says. She shivers excitedly. "Knowing King Ingram is dead and that an alliance between the two kingdoms is coming, I hardly slept a wink last night."

"Yes, and it shows," Pen says, without malice. I dare to say she sounds sympathetic; perhaps the knowledge of Nim's state has made her take pity. "You'll be no good to either kingdom if you drop from exhaustion. Take a nap."

Celeste blinks, surprised by the concern. "I suppose there isn't much else to do until my brother comes back with an update."

Hesitantly, she retires to her bedroom, leaving Pen and me alone.

"I truly believe she's going to kill herself with stress," Pen says. "What's the king's plan? He can hide Nim from her for only so long. She's going to want to know where he is when she's giving birth."

"I think he's hoping she'll forget about him."

"He must not know much about love, then," Pen says. "Or his daughter."

"I would believe that."

Pen moves to sit beside me, rests her head on my shoulder, and weaves her arm around mine. "Whatever happens now, I'm just so glad you're okay. I didn't know what would become of you after you left."

"I spoke with your father," I say. I feel her body tense. "I didn't tell him what I knew. But, Pen, he's valuable to King Furlow. And to Nim. He knew about the plans to assassinate King Ingram."

"That doesn't surprise me," Pen says, and it's as though she's speaking about a stain on her skirt. "He is head engineer and all that. The king has always favored him."

"You won't have to go back to him. Not ever again. Things are different now."

She pulls away from me and sits upright. "I'm not afraid of my father. I told you." She's focused on a crease in her skirt, and she works to smooth it.

"Pen—"

She looks at me. "The royals don't drink tonic, did you know? Internment's king must be ready to make a decision at a moment's notice. The queen and their children must also be ready, in case there's a death that leaves them in charge. So there's not a drop of tonic to be found in this apartment, and this isn't a conversation I wish to have unless I am very drunk."

I put my hand over hers. "All right. I'm sorry."

"Besides," she says with more verve, "we have enough problems to contend with, don't we? For starters, I nearly missed your wedding." She laughs at the absurdity of it and I do too.

I tell her about the fight Basil and I had after I told him about Judas, and the clumsy reconciliation. It's nice, really, to have normal problems and to pretend a fight with my betrothed is the most harrowing thing in my world.

"I'm relieved that the jet landed when it did," I blurt. "It isn't that I want to be with anyone other than Basil; it's just, after all of this, I want it to be my choice. And I know him; I know that he didn't want it to happen that way, either." I look uncertainly at the floor and then back to her. "Does that make me sound awfully selfish?"

She gives a wan smile. "No," she says. "Internment is frozen in time. Down on the ground, girls have already broken free. That's why we saw all those brilliant night clubs, and why the harbor was so alive at night. Marriage is fine and safe and nice, but there's so much else to do with our youth."

"I never thought I'd hear you say that Internment is frozen in time," I say. "Whenever I would talk about the ground before all of this, you'd try to shut me up."

"I was frightened," she confesses. "I love this city and I always will. It's my home. But I thought that if I understood its laws and I believed hard enough, no matter what I endured in life, things would always settle right side up in the end. I see now how small this place is. I was treating it like a god, but it's only a city."

"A magical floating city," I say, and we both laugh.

"I thought that being away from Internment would kill us. I thought it would make me question the god in the sky and everything we've been taught—and it has. I do question everything. But I want to have my questions. I want to have more thoughts than my mind can hold, so many that I have to write them in fragments like a madman."

"How much madder do you want to get?" I say.

She only smiles.

It takes nearly two weeks for the trains to resume running. The fence is repaired, and patrolmen are stationed all along it at every section to deter trespassers. Basil, Pen, Thomas, and I are free to roam the kingdom again, and though we're frequently bombarded with questions about the ground, no one seems to wish us harm.

Basil and Thomas are reunited with their families. I tell Basil that he should return home to them, but while he spends much of his days with his family, still he chooses to spend his nights with me in the clock tower. I want to look after Celeste, who is homebound and desperately lonely.

Pen doesn't return home at all, not even to see her mother, despite all her worrying. She doesn't say as much, but I know that she's afraid of being pulled back into that place again, and that this time she won't be able to leave. Pen's mother should have been the one protecting her, but it was always the other way around.

When I'm not being asked about Havalais, people ask me about the princess. They want to know if the rumors that she's dying are true. I smile and say that she's on the mend.

This is my only lie. Even Celeste's spirits have begun to drop, and she looks worse than ever. She has not been allowed to so much as step outside, not even within the confines of the royal gardens, since the jet returned, because the king is so terrified that someone will spot her. Her own mother's rapid decline and the months of isolation have begun to break her spirit, a spirit I once thought impenetrable.

One afternoon, when she's too exhausted to be up and about, I sit at her bedside and read to her. There must be a storm below us, because the clouds are especially thick and gray. Her still-bright eyes focus on the window and I know that she's missing the rain; it's one of her favorite wonders. She's tethered to that world below us forever now.

"Morgan." She interrupts me, and the words I was reading fade away. "Nim is in trouble. Isn't he?"

"No," I say. "I saw him just last night. Your father won't allow him to see you, and he is quite angry you both went over his head, but that's what you expected, isn't it?"

"I'm not that blind," she says, and pushes herself upright, her hands smoothing over her stomach like it's a globe filled with all the places she wishes to see. "My father has a cruel side. My brother and I have known since we were children. But we thought, 'Papa loves us, so he must be a good man. We'll understand one day.'"

"Don't you still believe that?" I say.

She shakes her head. "I'm not a child anymore," she says.

"I don't believe things simply because I want them to be so."

She winces at a stab of pain. They've been happening now for days. She should be in a hospital; even Prince Azure has told his father as much, but the king refuses. Whether it's for fear of his daughter's safety or fear of losing control of his own kingdom if anyone finds out about this child of two worlds, I don't know. But I suspect the latter. I fear he would let her die in childbirth from lack of care if it meant keeping the child a secret.

"Is there anything I can get you?" I say. "Have you had anything to drink today, at least?"

She closes her eyes for a long moment, and I can see that she's still in pain. "Find my brother," she says. "Make sure he's alone." As I stand, she grips my arm. "Don't let my father know."

"I won't. I'll be right back, I promise." She tightens her grip before she releases it. "I promise," I say again, to convince myself as well.

She doesn't ask me to find Nimble. She knows it would be no use. He would already be by her side if he were free.

I hurry down the steps, through the lobby that is only sparsely populated by people collecting their wages, and make my way down the set of halls that leads to the basement. The prince has been busy these past two weeks, playing his father's politics and overseeing the prisoners. He interviews the men from the ground every day, testing their potential loyalty. I can see all the while that his heart isn't in it. He and his sister have lost whatever respect they held for their father, and have even come to fear him.

While Celeste has begun evading her father, Prince Azure has grown disdainful of him. He doesn't say as much, but I can see it in the way he speaks to the prisoners, as though he sympathized with their anger at being trapped here, as though he knew of a less barbaric way to handle this if only he were king.

But I see it especially in the way he cares for Nimble Piper, spooning water into his mouth when his jaw is clamped shut, whispering that he must get better for the sake of his own kingdom.

When I open the basement door, I find the prince sitting on the top step, pale, exasperated, staring down into the darkness. He barely offers me a glance.

"They never tire of orders," he says. "Our patrolmen. They can't live without someone telling them what to do. It's all so exhausting, having to think for them."

I would love to argue against this. My father, at least, was one who did not accept orders without question. But there's no time. "You have to get to Celeste," I say, trying to catch my breath. "She's in pain again. I think—" I look around to be sure we're alone, and then I whisper, "I think it's time."

He's on his feet in an instant, his self-pitying fatigue gone. He rushes past me, and I follow him up the stairs and into the apartment.

Celeste has tumbled out of bed and she's standing with her hands pressed against the window ledge, head down, struggling to draw even breaths. Her bedsheets are dampened through.

"Leste." The prince is gasping for air, but he's gentle when he wraps his arm around her shoulders and brings her back to the bed. "I'm right here. What do you need?"

She shakes her head. "I don't know! I thought Nim would be here for this. I thought I would be prepared." She shudders with pain.

"Leste, listen to me. I'm going to send for our doctor. It's going to be fine. The doctor will know exactly what to do."

"You can't," she sobs. "Papa will try to take the baby away. He'll put it wherever he's put Nim."

"I won't let him. I won't." He's speaking so calmly, like he's reading a bedtime story to a child. "I'll be right back."

"No!" She's clinging to his arm as he stands. "Please!"

"Don't be stupid," he says. "I've gone along with this plan of yours—not that I've had any choice in the matter—but I won't let you do this without a doctor."

Her fingers are digging into his skin, and he has to wrench himself free. "Az!" She doubles over with pain, and I see the anguish on his face as he rushes past me. I could swear there were tears in his eyes.

I have never seen Celeste so hysterical. It's the fear, not the pain, that's doing it. I sit beside her at the edge of the bed, and I don't speak in dulcet tones, I don't try to console her. I know that she won't believe me.

It's an eternity before the prince returns, a doctor in tow. He's a small man with hair that's severely slicked back, and he's much older than any doctor who would be allowed to practice. The prince surely pulled him out of dodder housing.

"Strip the bed," he tells me, and his tone is so icy and

authoritative, I oblige quickly and with shaking hands. He opens his medical bag and produces a flame generator used for cooking in apartments without electricity. He sends me away to fill a pot with water.

My mind is spinning. After I've brought the water, I'm not allowed back into the room. I sit on the floor in the hallway, staring at an oil coloring of the prince and princess as children, arm in arm in their finest white dress.

"Doctor O. has been with our family for years," Prince Azure says as he comes out of his sister's room. Exiled as well, no doubt. "He's the doctor who saw to our genders before we were in the womb. He's the one who delivered us."

The prince is known for his poise, but now he drops to the floor across from me, his arm draped over his angled knee, and he looks as though he could melt into the floorboards. "A curious thing, isn't it? Our genders being determined even before we're born. The king and queen wanted an heir and a spare, and they knew just how we should be assembled. They ordered us as though we were items on a menu."

He nods to his sister's closed door. "Sometimes I think we were born all wrong, my sister and I. Sure, we know how to dress the part, but we have our own wild ideas about what we would do if the kingdom were left to us.

"I'm better at playing along. I pretend I'll be the king my father wants me to be. I say yes and I go along, knowing I can rule my own way once it's my turn. My sister has no patience for that. No sense of strategy. She's always been stupidly impulsive. But I never thought she would take it this far."

I say nothing. He isn't seeking words of comfort. There's a pained cry from the other side of the door, and he bows his head.

"This baby will merge two worlds, won't it?" he says, with a humorless laugh. "But it has to get here the same grotesque way the rest of us did."

Celeste shouldn't be alone on that soiled mattress. She should be in a hospital, surrounded by electricity and nurses. Nim should be beside her. She was so small and frightened when I left her.

I strain my ears to listen, but I can hear nothing on the other side of the door now.

"This is typical of her," the prince says. I can hear the worry under his cool tone. "She doesn't think things *through*. How am I supposed to pull her out of this one?"

"I think the whole point is that you can't," I say. I pause to see if my boldness has offended him, but he's listening. "She didn't want you to save her. She's never wanted to be saved. She had it in her mind that she was going to do this, and it can't be undone."

"I think you're right about that," he says. I have seen the prince dozens of times in regal sketches, at festivities, and on broadcasts, and this is the first time I look at him and truly see an equal. A person as powerless as the rest of us.

"My sister thought that our father would come around, that he would see what she was doing for the kingdoms and accept this child of two worlds. She's always believed he loves us more than he does."

"Perhaps he will, with time," I try.

"No," he says. "Papa was livid. The only reason he didn't hold her down himself and force her to have a termination procedure is because it was too late by then. She'd have bled to death." The words are horrible, but he's so utterly drained that he can speak only frankly. "Once the child is born, he has asked me to drown it like a double birth. And then it will be as though this never happened. There's to be no love story for my sister and that boy from the ground. She'll be lucky if she sees daylight again before her eighteenth birthday, when she's married off to her betrothed."

Though I suspected something like this, it nauseates me. My heart is pounding. "You can't let that happen."

He looks at me, that trademark royal brightness in his eyes. "I have a plan I've been working out, but I'll need you to prove to me that you're competent," he says, and I should be offended but I find his familiar cockiness to be a sign that things will be all right again. "I'll need you to go to the prison and create a diversion. Get Nimble Piper out of there through the back entrance."

"The one that leads to the plum court?"

"Yes, the very same. Here—" He hurries down the hall and returns with a scrap of paper and a pen. He sketches a crude map of the woods surrounding the clock tower. "There are several stone caverns off the trails. Hide him there. Stay with him and wait for me."

"How long?" I ask.

"I don't know how bloody long. However long it takes babies to be born."

"But Basil and Pen," I say.

"What about them?"

"If you're asking me to betray the king, and I'm certain you are, I need to know that they won't be punished on my behalf."

"You do this for me, and I'll make certain they're someplace safe. You have my word."

A scream from beyond the closed door makes us both wince. "What about Celeste?" I say.

"What about her? She can't very well go sneaking away into the woods right now, can she?" His face has paled considerably. "I'll look after her. But I can't be everywhere. Morgan, I need you."

There's a set of words I never expected to hear from him, but all I say is, "What kind of diversion?"

"It will have to be something that requires the attention of every patrolman. Tell them—tell them my father has been wounded. Say that he's been stabbed by a citizen who's been maddened by the edge or some such. After weeks being cooped up down in the cellar, they're all just itching to be heroes. Go on now, go." He fumbles with the key ring and extracts the key to Nim's cell. "Don't get caught. I can't afford to save you too."

I nod. I hurry through the apartment before I'm made to listen to another scream. I couldn't bear it. The prince is left rooted to the hallway, his sister struggling behind one door, his mother dying behind another.

His diversion works. The patrolmen are so lost and desperate for their leader that when I tell them the king has been harmed, they are eager to rush to the king's side. They pay me no mind as they hurry past.

My hands are shaking as I work the key into the lock. I drop it twice. When I finally get the door open, I find Nim sitting up against the wall. He was dozing in a fitful sleep, but his face registers alertness when he sees me.

"Morgan?" His voice is hoarse, his lips cracked and bloody. But he does look better than he did the last time I was down here. "Is it really you? Is Celeste—"

"Can you stand?" I work the key through the lock on his restraints, and they fall away. He clenches his fists. "Come on. There isn't time." I pull him to his feet and position him so that he can rest on my shoulder as we walk. He stumbles dizzily.

"Wait," he says. He's delirious. I can feel the heat of his fever when he drops his face against my neck.

"We can't wait. We have only a few minutes before the patrolmen realize they've been tricked. They'll be combing the entire city looking for us."

I don't think he hears my explanation. He's scarcely conscious.

All I am thinking as I drag him from the clock tower and into the woods is that I won't allow him to die on the day when his child is born.

18

I sit huddled in a cavern much like the one Pen and I claimed as our sanctuary. This place feels familiar even though it's the royal family's private property, where the prince and princess do their hunting for sport.

Or they used to, at least.

Nim weaves in and out of consciousness. In his brief lucid moments, I tell him that we're someplace safe and that the others will be with us soon. I tell him over and over, reassuring myself as well.

Before the ground was ever introduced to our city, these woods would have been lined by patrolmen keeping trespassers away, but now there's only the rustle of leaves and a chilly breeze that comes along with the short season.

It was sometime past noon when I left Celeste at the hands of that doctor with the soulless eyes. Now the sun has melted below the city's edge and stars have begun to show themselves.

I wonder if her child has been born. I wonder if Prince Azure has managed to keep it alive.

Nimble stirs. He reaches out and touches my arm. "Birdie?"

"No," I say. "It's me. Morgan."

He struggles to sit upright and I help him. The prince was giving him sedatives to help with the pain, and now he's starting to emerge for the first time in weeks. Awareness is starting to show in his eyes. "Do you know where you are?" I ask.

He looks over my shoulder, at the darkening sky. "Internment," he says. "I was in prison."

"Yes." Hope fills me. "Yes, and you're out now."

"Where's Celeste?" he says. "I have to go to her. You have to take me."

"Soon," I say, uncertain whether I'm lying. He's already in so much pain, I don't want to add to that the pain of uncertainty.

But after weeks of a medicated haze, Nim isn't having it. He's awake now. "What's happened to her?"

He tries to climb out of the cavern, and I hold his shoulders down. "She's having the baby now. Or maybe she already has—it's been hours since I've seen her. Prince Azure is with her."

"I have to get to her." His voice is desperate. For all his injuries, he's found the strength to fight me off when I try to keep him down. He scrambles out of the cavern and starts pacing furiously through the trees.

"Nim," I whisper harshly. "You can't. The king will have patrolmen looking for us. If we're caught, it's all over."

"She needs me!"

I grab his arm, and he stumbles, still dizzy. "Yes, she needs you. She needs you outside of a prison cell, and more important, she needs you alive. I can't promise either of those things if you go bursting into the clock tower demanding to see her."

He looks helplessly into the distance. He wouldn't know how to get to the clock tower even if I did let him go. "The prince won't let anything happen to her."

Nim shakes his head. "She wanted to believe the best of her father, but I knew—I knew he would put her in danger. Her and the baby."

I drop my arms to my sides. "What did you expect, Nim? You've got royal blood; you've seen how kings are. They don't like having their position challenged, much less by an infant."

He stumbles forward and catches himself against a tree. He's breathing hard, teeth gritted. In his urgency to get to Celeste he forgot about his injuries, but the pain has reminded him now.

"All we can do is wait for word from the prince," I tell him. "I'm sorry."

He limps back to the cavern, utterly defeated, and hits the rock face in frustration. Almost in tandem with the motion, there's a sound within the depth of the woods. A creak. I push Nimble into the shadows of the cavern and follow after him and hold my breath.

It was foolish of us to speak as loudly as we did. Patrolmen will be looking for us by now.

I hear the noise again, not so much a creak as a whimper. A figure emerges from the trees, and it whispers my name.

Prince Azure. His steps were silent, not so much as a rustle of leaves or the snap of a twig, expert hunter that he is, but that whimpering persists, and as he gets closer, I realize that he's holding something in his arms.

"Morgan!" he whispers.

I crawl out of the cavern. "I'm here."

Nim is rushing to get past me, but before he can make it to his feet, the prince has knelt down before us. The bundle in his arms is moving, and it gives out a feeble croak.

Nim gasps. "It's—"

"Yes, yes," the prince says, like he's bored with the whole thing. "It's a girl, born just a few moments ago. Perfectly healthy from what I can see, but I'm no doctor."

"Is it safe for a newborn to be outside like this?" I say, marveling despite myself at its pale face like a faded little moon in the darkness. "There's a chill in the air."

"Safer outside than inside," the prince says. "My father thinks I've taken her outside to drown her in the ravine."

Nim is shaking when he reaches for the infant, but the prince hands her to me. He's perhaps still too untrusting of this boy from the ground.

I hold the infant, feel her slight bit of weight. The next generation of an ancient royal lineage in my arms.

Instinctively I raise the blanket up past her ears to keep out the chill.

"I'll escort you to the jet," the prince says. "I've been interrogating men from the ground and there are three whom I trust to fly you back to the ground."

"The ground," I echo dumbly. "But Basil—"

"He's already there waiting for you. Your loudmouthed blond friend too. See? I keep my promises."

Nimble is staring at the child. His child. He surely has a million questions, but all he says is, "What about Celeste?"

"What about her?" the prince says, exasperated.

"Is she coming with us?"

"No, she's not coming. Don't be a moron. She's so heavily sedated, she wouldn't know her own name if you asked her."

"I'm not leaving without her," Nim says.

"Suit yourself." The price rises to a stand. "But that baby is leaving this city tonight, if you want it to survive."

I move to follow the prince, and Nim grabs my sleeve. "Morgan."

"He's right," I say, with all my sympathy. "I can't make you come along, but I think you should. Celeste would want you to take care of your kingdom. You'll find your way back to each other again; of course you will."

Nim looks up at the prince. "You claim to keep your promises. I need your word that Celeste will be safe."

"She's not the one in danger," the prince says.

Hesitantly, Nim moves to follow, and in a rare display, the prince helps pull Nim to his feet. Prince Azure doesn't wait for us, though, before he moves forward into the darkness.

The prince has a hunter's stride. Silent, graceful. Nim struggles to keep up, panting and clutching his wounds.

The infant is mercifully quiet, unfazed by the ordeal of her birth and the great trouble it has caused.

We move through the agriculture section, away from the city's lights. We cross the train tracks, and Prince Azure cuts through the fence with his hunting knife and makes an opening that I can duck through.

"There was nowhere to hide the jet," the prince says. "My father had it moved out here. Everyone's afraid of the thing, even his patrolmen, which is silly if you ask me. It's only a machine."

There was once a time when I feared this side of the tracks. Now I see that it's only grass and starlight. No maddening song on the wind to lure me over. I still remember exactly who I am and what's worth fighting for.

Nim stops to catch his breath, and I let him lean on my shoulder for support. For all his panting and cringing, he stares in awe at the stars, as though he could reach out and pluck them from the sky.

"This is your world," he says, breathless. "This has been floating above me all my life."

"Yes," the prince says. "It's a pity you can't see more of it, but we really must be going."

"Come on," I tell him. "I can see the jet just ahead."

And I can, though there is nothing but starlight to illuminate its dusky, tarnished body. It's hard to believe this battered thing will have enough life left in it to take Nimble and his new child home, but I have to believe it will.

The metal door swings open, revealing a mouth of darkness. But the darkness isn't complete; I can see the outline of blond curls. As we move closer, I can see Pen more clearly. She's standing as still as a statue in the doorway, with her hand gripping the doorframe.

Her eyes move to the infant, and then to Nim. Her lips part, and I can see the faint tremble in her lower lip. She glances sidelong into the jet as though someone is speaking to her.

This isn't right.

"What in the world are you gawking at?" the prince asks her.

"Pen?" I say.

Her mouth forms a word. She whispers it at first, and then she yells it, "Run!"

Only then do I see the king standing behind her in the darkness. He brings his face close to hers, and I can see his pale, tired complexion. He says something to her through gritted teeth, and she yells again, "Run, Morgan. He'll kill you!"

They're the last words she's able to say. Before I can move in one direction or the other, the king has slashed her throat.

19

My scream could surely wake the dead in the tributary.

A clean line of blood appears, thin and even, then dripping. Pen drops to the ground, and I can swear I see her chest rising with a breath when the king kicks her away, into that unyielding blackness.

In my arms, the infant has begun screaming, a shrill cry that's scarcely human. All I can think is that I want her to stop, so I can listen for Pen's breathing, and for Basil, who is surely calling for me. He must be in that jet. He must be injured, or he would come to me now. He would never have let that happen to Pen.

I don't let myself think that either of them could be dead. I won't, until I can see them for myself. I run for the jet, and Nimble is the one to stop me, only as long as it takes for him to grab his daughter from my arms. He no longer has the strength to stand, and he collapses into a kneel, clutching her like life itself.

The prince stands before the two of them protectively.

The king comes toward him like a mad beast, but we're madder, Nimble and the prince and I. The king of Internment, for all his schemes and ploys, may love this city with all his decaying heart, but he will never know the power of loving more important things.

I have seen too many killed, I have lost too much, and I will not lose another thing at his hand. He is brandishing something in his grip—another weapon perhaps. I try to grab it, but I am of no interest to him and he shoves me out of his way.

I'm insubstantial, like his foolish daughter. His son is the one he means to subdue. When the king reaches Prince Azure, he raises something that I believe at first to be the knife. But when he plunges it into the prince's neck, there is no blood.

The prince drops to the ground, his eyes still open and blinking, a tranquilizer dart jutting from his skin.

Perhaps the king truly does love the prince more than the prince could believe. He didn't kill him.

Prince Azure's eyes are on me, and as I meet them, I see what I could swear is permission. The king pays me no mind. Now that he's removed his most immediate threat, he wants the thing he's come to kill—his grandchild.

Nim is struggling to get to his feet. He's broken and tired, and he's just walked hundreds of paces, but whatever is left in him, he'll give. The king knows it isn't much.

It's almost done. He can toss the infant into the edge and she'll bounce back, broken and dead. What's to stop him? There's nothing here. Just me, sobbing and shaking.

When I lunge for the knife that's still in his hand, he isn't expecting it and he gives a startled cry. He's got such a firm grasp on the hilt that I have to grab it by the blade. I feel it slicing into my skin.

He elbows me in the stomach, but to my own surprise I'm laughing, even as the pain hits. He has ruled this floating city for all these years, and all he has to defend it with is a knife.

Blood has made my palm and wrist sticky, and I don't know whether it's his blood or mine. With a punishing shove he manages to throw me to the ground.

The struggle has given Nim enough of an advance. He's gone, but the persistent wail of the infant tells me that he's in the jet. I get a glance and see that the door has been pulled shut.

Nim and that infant may be it, the only ones who will survive this night.

I'm in the dirt, and if the king didn't pay me any mind before, he certainly does now. He's straddled over me, blood smeared on his shirt. Pen's, perhaps, or mine. It could be Basil's, for all I know, but my mind won't allow me to believe it. For all I've been made to believe in the past year, I will not believe that my betrothed and my best friend are gone.

I grab the king's wrist, and the knife is hovering over my face, shaking uncertainly, as though the blade itself isn't sure which of us to kill.

The king drives his knee into my stomach and I see it for just a moment—the fear in his eyes that I may have something in me after all, that I won't die so easily.

The jet's engines splutter and then roar to life. Dirt splashes my face, and the king raises his head. While he's been busy with me, the boy he wounded has gotten away. Nim is going to make it. He's going to fly to the ground and take his place as king, him and his child of two worlds.

The moment's distraction is all I need. I grab the knife from the king's faltered grip and I plunge it into his throat.

Blood rains onto my face, some of it landing in my mouth, and I splutter and cough as I push myself away from him. Despite my hatred, I cannot look at him as he dies. I hear him struggling in the grass, and I turn to the stars. They are oblivious to my existence on this small, floating rock, and yet I've known them all my life. If they cared at all for living things, I believe they would understand what I have done.

The king ceases to struggle. I don't know that I believe in the tributary anymore, if I ever did, but if there is any good in him at all to go there, it's the part that loved his children and his kingdom. Though he betrayed them, though he did deplorable things, it was the best he had to offer.

The taste of his blood makes me vomit in the grass, and even after I recover, I'm still trembling when I get to my feet. I'm only distantly aware of a pain in my hand and chest. No matter. There's no time for that now. The jet is still here, and there's still a chance that Prince Azure and I can be on it.

"Your Majesty," I say when I kneel at the prince's side. His eyes are dull and glassy, but he's breathing and I know he can hear me. I remove the tranquilizer from his neck. "You have to wake up," I tell him. "You're the king."

The words feel very far away. The prince-turned-king blurs, and a pair of arms catches me as I fall back.

My eyes close, and I don't have the strength to open them, but that's no matter. I'd recognize Basil's touch anywhere.

Motion. He's bringing me to my feet. My mind registers the feel of the metal steps reverberating under my shoes. I double over, sick in the grass a second time. He picks me up again when I'm through. I hear my own heavy breathing, taste the blood. Something is screaming, screeching like the seagulls that flew along the shoreline of Havalais.

Darkness.

When I am able to open my eyes again, I'm certain that days have passed. But the starlight is still streaming through the jet's window, and I realize, heart sinking, that we have not gone anywhere.

"Hey." Basil's voice is eager. He holds my arm, keeping me steady. I'm in one of the jet's seats and everything spins when I try to move. "You need to be still. You've lost a lot of blood," he says.

"Where's Pen?" I don't dare look at his face. Before he can answer, I force myself to ask, "The king killed her, didn't he?"

A laugh, weary yet assured. That's when my vision

comes back into focus and I see that Pen is sitting across from me, her blood-soaked shirtsleeve tied around her collar. "It's going to take more than that," she says.

I open my mouth to speak, but a sob comes out instead. I lean against Basil, who frets and smoothes back my hair. "I thought you were both dead," I say.

"Please. He hardly got me," Pen says, panting from the effort of speaking. "Couldn't find an artery if there were an arrow pointing to it. Suppose that's why his men did all the killing for him."

"But I saw you go down," I say.

"A tip, Morgan: If someone tries to slit your throat, and you're fortunate enough that they've failed, you let them think they've succeeded."

I reach out and take her hand. Sometime later, after we are all safe and rested and bathed, I should like to collapse into a good and relieved fit of tears.

"He tranquilized me and propped me up against the wall there," Basil says. "He said he wanted me to see what happened to traitors and bastards born outside of the queue, that men needed to learn about death before they could be of any use."

Pen scoffs, but I see the wince of pain she tries to hide.

"Nim?" I say. "The baby?"

"Both asleep at the helm, remarkably," Pen says. "He wasn't going to leave without you. He wanted to create a diversion by starting the engines."

"Prince Azure?" I say. "Or I suppose he's the new King Furlow now."

"Still out cold. I couldn't move him," Basil says. "His dart must have been stronger."

The thought of Prince Azure lying paralyzed in the grass, mere paces from his father's body, is too much for me to take. With great effort I pull myself to my feet. My hand is wrapped in scraps that are presumably from Basil's torn sleeves.

A pain in my shoulder flares to life. So the king did manage to wound me after all. Basil does not try to stop me, but rather stands behind me, steadying me when I sway one way and then the other, like one who's had too much tonic.

I descend the stairs slowly, Basil's grip on my arm the strongest thing I've ever known.

"It's bad, isn't it?" I say. "Pen's wound."

"I'm convinced she's immortal," Basil says.

"She needs to see a doctor, and Nim, and that baby. Basil, a newborn shouldn't be out like this."

"Nor should you, in this shape," Basil says. "But we're all strong to the point of being stupid, aren't we?"

I laugh, and the pain in my shoulder intensifies. I don't look at the king's body as we pass it, but Basil does, though he says nothing of my gruesome handiwork.

I drop to a kneel at the prince's side. "Your Majesty," I say, for the second time. His eyes open and his fingers twitch. He struggles to speak, opening and closing his mouth and groaning before he gets the word out. "Havalais."

I think he means it to be a question. "No," I say. "You're still on Internment."

He falls unconscious again, for once a victim of those

tranquilizer darts the royal family so favors.

"Should I try to drag him onto the jet?" Basil asks.

"No point," I say. "He needs to stay here and assume his place as king, and we ought to hear his ruling, shouldn't we?"

"Do you suppose it would be in our favor?" Basil asks. "He never did seem to like us. Or Nim."

"No, but he loves Internment. He'll do right by it. I hope."

I stay by Prince Azure's side through the night, weaving in and out of consciousness. Basil sits up in the grass beside me, always awake, keeping watch.

It's the baby's cries that startle us all awake, sometime before dawn. The sound could replace the clock tower's hourly trills, for it's surely being heard through every window in the city.

Prince Azure sits up, wincing, clutching his sore back and neck, shrugging his shoulders. "Are we still here?" he says sourly. "After all that?"

Pen staggers to the door of the jet and has to yell over the baby's cries. "It's not going to shut up, you know. It's hungry." The concept of motherhood has always eluded her and this experience is reinforcing her disdain.

"What do you propose I do about it?" Prince Azure asks her.

"Don't ask me," she fires back. "You're the king."

20

I don't retain most of the walk back to the clock
tower. I black out for moments at a time, but somehow my
legs keep moving.

Prince Azure leads the way, saying nothing. The sun is
rising now, making the city pink and gold. It's his first day
as king, and he does not seem happy to see it.

My knees buckle, and when Basil can't hold me up,
he kneels alongside me. The clock tower is in sight now,
but as I look up at it, it may as well be a world away. It is
Havalais's harbor glittering on the other side of the sea.

"She can't go any farther," Pen says, and drops her arms
like dead weight. "She needs to be in a hospital." She needs
a doctor as much as I do, but she doesn't say that.

The prince turns to face the lot of us, the infant cradled
in his arm. How he managed to silence her is a wonder.
Maybe she was born with her own political agenda; it certainly wouldn't surprise me.

"Morgan," the prince says. "You're very tired, and maybe you don't remember what happened back there, so I'll remind you."

I raise my eyes to look at him. My vision is tunneling.

"When we made it to the jet, my father the king was there to see us off. He was sending us to Havalais with his blessing. But one of his patrolmen was maddened from being so close to the edge, and he killed my father. He tried to kill us all, but you managed to wrestle the knife away and kill him instead. You did it to save us. That's what happened, do you understand?"

"Yes," I say.

"I'm glad we're in agreement," he says. "My sister will want a full report and that is what I intend to tell her. Best to leave the details to me. I have the clearest memory of the scuffle."

The infant has begun screaming again. Hungry, cold, nameless. *She ought to be back with her mother,* I think, before my vision goes dark and I fall into silence.

When I sleep, I have a dream that doesn't belong to me. Rather, it's something that has been haunting my brother for years. He told me about it weeks ago, though it all seems like a lifetime away now.

In the dream, Internment is the same as it has always been. I step over the train tracks and suddenly I'm at the edge, staring down at the ground that reveals itself through wisps of clouds.

I don't want to jump. I only want to have a better look. I

lean forward, and my feet are pulled from the ground. Then I'm weightless, careening away from the clouds, away from my answers.

When darkness takes over, it isn't perfect. A heart beats inside it, and I can almost make out the shape of some small and living thing—almost.

"Wait," I say, for it is being pulled out of my reach. "I know who you belong to."

But it doesn't listen. Willing the past to be undone, even in dreams, can't set things right again. All I can say is, "Come back. Come back. Come back," until it is gone.

In the darkness I hear a cry, and I think that I've succeeded, that it has heard me and I will return what has been stolen from my brother. From Alice.

But the cry is not coming from within my dream. It's in the waking world, finding its way to my ears. It belongs to a different life entirely, one that may have a chance yet. We've all fought so hard for it.

I'm in the hospital for the better part of a week. I'm well enough to leave, but I hesitate to leave Nimble and Pen in this awful hospital alone. Though Pen put forth a brave face, she and Nimble bore the worst of it. They've both been scarcely conscious since we got here.

It was only after I began to improve that Basil relented when I told him that his time would be better spent helping the new king and visiting with his family. I know how awful it is to be a visitor in a place like this, and I wish for him to not experience it.

Though Pen was fortunate enough that the king's wound did not prove fatal, it fast became infected and she's been bedridden with fever. I've exaggerated my own injuries just to stay on this floor and be near her. But that can last only so long. A patrolman came to my room to inform me that the king has requested I have an audience with him at noon.

The only consolation is that, under the orders of the king, Pen's and Nimble's rooms are to be guarded at all times, in case anyone may try to cause them harm. No visitors are permitted into this area at all. Not even family or Thomas. Not even Pen's father.

When I visit Pen, her face gleams with perspiration and she's flushed with fever, but determined to stay awake. I think her nightmares of the harbor bombing still haunt her. They surely still haunt me.

I sit in the chair by her bed, and she offers me a wan smile. "You look dreadfully glum," she says.

"I just hate to see you like this," I say.

"Me? I'm fine." She looks to the window, and there are clouds reflected in her green eyes. "I've had plenty of time to think about things."

"You shouldn't be thinking," I say. "You should be resting."

"A girl should never stop thinking," she says. "Otherwise we'll become what our world thinks of us." She's struggling to keep her eyes open. "Dull, simple creatures that must belong to someone lest we hurt ourselves."

I push the sweaty hair from her face. Without her neat curls or glossy plaits, she looks almost like a stranger.

"Oh, Morgan, stop," she pleads. "I can't stand it when you worry so much about me. Really. The look on your face."

"It is taxing being your friend. I worry about you constantly."

She pushes herself upright. "What about you?" She lowers her voice. "You haven't been sleeping. I hear you pass my door a dozen times a night."

"I'm all right," I say.

"Are you, then?" She has a way of staring through me. I've always been a dreadful liar, but I'm trying, for her sake. Her mouth twists, and she looks to the window. "What was it like?" she asks, in a low voice. "Killing him."

"It doesn't matter," I say, all too quickly.

"Of course it matters."

Suddenly the sharp sterile odor of the room turns my mouth dry. My palms are slick and I rub them against my gown as though I could clean it all away that easily.

Pen is looking at me now, offering me no reprieve. She means for me to admit it. "He was going to kill me," I say. "All of us. He was going to kill his own grandchild."

I hate her silence. I stare at the floor. "I had to. That's all. I don't know what more you want."

"You see him when you close your eyes," she says. "Don't you? When you sleep?"

Numbly, I nod. "But I still kill him, even in my dreams," I say. "I have it to do over, and I do, again and again. That's how I know I had to."

The king dies again in the silence that passes just then, the blood black in the starlight, the whites of his eyes dimming like a spent bulb. The only reprieve was the soft sounds of the grass, as though the city wanted to say it forgave me. Thanked me, even.

"I've killed in my dreams, too," Pen says. Her eyes are fixed on the window. She won't look at me, but she won't look down the way that I do. She has had years to grow familiar with the sort of hatred it takes to kill.

"I know that I'm dreaming, in some way, but every time, when he comes into my room and I finally move to kill him, I will it to be real. I think that if I want it enough, I can somehow change the rules about what a dream alone can do." I see the coldness in her eyes that makes me hate the one who did this to her, made her think such things. "Then I wake up, and this world and its consequences race back into my head as though they've been hovering over my pillow waiting for me to come back. And I know that I can't kill him—not without suffering tenfold for it. I learned a long time ago that if I want him to be dead, he's dead. He can't have my thoughts when I'm awake. He can't make his darkness be my darkness."

She runs her hands over the blankets, smoothing the wrinkles. "Still, though. I've wondered how it would feel. If I'd get any satisfaction."

For all the king did, and even though he tried to dispose of me the way he did my parents, I still can't bring myself to hate him as much as I hate Pen's father. The king, in his way, believed he was protecting his kingdom. He believed he was doing something noble. But Pen's father meant only to take something that was not meant to be given. He gave no mind to his daughter, no mind to the way he would change the world as she saw it, even when she was older and stronger. The brilliant thoughts in her head that he pervaded. The tonic forcing itself into her blood the way he forced himself into her, just so she can find solace from him for a few meager hours.

He is a different kind of murderer, and there is nothing in him that can be redeemed.

"I wish your dreams could be real, too," I say.

She moves across the bed and rests her head against my shoulder. I feel all the weight go out of her, and she closes her eyes. For just a moment, she is the little girl I wasn't able to save all those years ago, and at last she allows someone to console her.

I kiss the crown of her head, and she puts her arms around my neck. Both of us killers, both of us murdered and brought back to life.

I'm not the only one pacing the halls of our tiny wing. On my way back to my bed, I find Nimble standing at the tiny window at the end of the hallway, staring at the glasslands in the distance.

He flinches when I stand beside him. "Sorry," I say.

"It isn't your fault," he says. "My nerves are fried." The city is reflected in his lenses. He shakes his head as though he can't believe it. "I expected a war-torn mess when I got here, but if you look away from all the digging and at the city itself, it's beautiful. Hardly what I think of when I imagine a city at all."

"Most of those buildings are hundreds of years old," I say. "We've outfitted them with electricity and plumbing, but the bones are the same. No reason to demolish them and make waste."

"No weather to wear away at them," he says.

I laugh. "I've gotten to know you so well, I almost forgot you're a foreigner here. Still, we aren't very different, are we?"

"No, we aren't," he agrees.

After a long silence, he says, "It doesn't feel real yet that I'm king. All my life it's felt so far away." He shakes his head. "I've always hated them—kings. Wasting away in their castles that could be better used a thousand other ways."

"It's your castle now," I say. "Who says it has to be a castle at all? It could be its own city."

He smiles, and his stare is faraway, as though he's imagining it. "Havalais doesn't know yet that the old king is dead. There are advisers handling affairs for me while I'm gone, and in secret, Birdie is advising them on my behalf. She's the only one I trust. If news got out that there is no formal leader, or that a broad is running the show in my absence, Dastor would be at an advantage. It was irresponsible of me to go, but I felt I had to."

"To see Celeste," I say.

"You make me sound like a lovesick kid."

"No shame in that."

"Maybe it's true," he says. "I did want to see her. I wanted to see her world. To see the city of Internment and the clock tower where she's lived as a princess, I can finally understand her optimism. Her faith in things."

Havalais is quite the opposite of Internment. What it lacks in modesty it makes up for in aggression. Even its beauty is aggressive, with bold music and bright lights and glamorous girls with black lips on silver screens. If Celeste is a product of her world, Nim is a rare creature in his own. All modesty and softness.

"I admit that I have a hard time seeing things the way she does," I say. "But I hope she's right. I hope our two kingdoms really can come together."

"There aren't many things I'm sure of," Nim says. "But I'm sure about that."

The new king is high up in his clock tower, in the royal apartment. He requests to see me alone. Even the patrolman who escorted me waits outside the door.

He's standing at the open window when I reach him, staring into the garden of poppies far below.

"You wanted to see me?" My voice is uncertain; now that he's had time to reflect, I don't know what he makes of his father's murder at my hand. This is the first time we've spoken since the melee.

"There's to be a ceremony," he says hollowly. "I'm king now, of course, living and breathing. But tradition dictates a ceremony. It's what my father did, and his father before him, and so on back to our first king."

"You haven't called me here to advise you on that, have you?" I say. "I wouldn't know how. Parties are best left to someone like your sister."

"Oh, believe me, she's got plenty of ideas about what I should wear." He turns to face me, his hands still braced on the window ledge. "I've called you to share one of my key ideas. Come over here, would you?"

Cautiously I approach the window, not entirely certain whether he means to push me through it.

But as I follow his gesture to look through it, he leans on his forearms and nods to the poppies far beneath us. "That was my sister's favorite place in the world when we were growing up. She was betrothed to a truly dreadful boy who also happened to be deathly allergic to most flowers. She'd run out to the center of the poppies with her skirts gathered, and she'd stand there taunting him as he demanded her affections."

"Sounds quite like her," I say.

"I admired her petulance toward him, and her bravery," he says. "But I also feared it. I thought that if she resisted, she'd be whisked off to one of those camps and that her brains would be scooped out with a spoon until she was nothing but a blubbering mass of compliance."

I look at him. "The attraction camps, you mean."

"Yes, right. I won't startle you with the gruesome details, but needless to say I hate it there—not only for what it is, but because it exists at all. So I'm going to do away with it. And that begins with getting rid of betrothals."

"Completely?" I say.

"I've always hated that tradition," he says. "Perhaps it works sometimes—you and your betrothed seem to get on rather well. But my sister chose that limping, haggard boy from Havalais. And what for? Because, as you've told me, he's kind. He's the opposite of what she was fated to as she fled to the poppies."

"He is," I agree.

"Would you still choose your betrothed if you had the option?"

"Yes," I say.

He gives me a wan smile. "I'm not questioning your loyalty to Internment's laws, Stockhour. It's an honest question. No need to be frightened."

Was I frightened? The quickness of my answer was a reflex, brought on by the interrogation my family endured after my brother jumped.

"It's not an easy question," I confess. "I've known my whole life that Basil and I were meant to be together. I don't know how I'd feel if we met only now for the first time, or if he and I had always just been classmates in a crowd. I can tell you only that I love him now as it is."

"I suspect many will feel the way you do, and that's fine," he says, and raises his chin as though he's come to an important decision that he's quite proud of. "But that shall be my first act as king. Keep your betrotheds if you want, but I'm doing away with that archaic custom."

"What about ensuring everyone gets a match?" I say. "What about the population?"

"Not everyone *wants* a match, and even if they do, they should be free to make that decision. Isn't that what they do on the ground?"

I shrug. "They have more space to roam. They do plenty

of things down there that I find maddening." Like a mother abandoning her children so that she might see the world without them.

"Yes, yes," he says. "I do think Internment could borrow a bit of their madness. I want to talk to your friend Margaret about the risks of opening a regular flight path to the ground."

"If you call her Margaret, she won't help you at all. It's Pen."

"Fine then. Pen. I asked to see her as well. Where is she?"

"She couldn't leave the hospital just yet. She's too ill."

"That won't do." He frowns out at his kingdom. "I'm going to need someone with a head for math and physics giving me counsel."

"Her father is the head engineer at the glasslands," I remind him, and though the idea of Pen's father being put in a position of power frightens me, he does know quite much about how the city is fueled.

"Never cared for him—too pleasant, like he's hiding bodies under the bed," he says. "Never cared for Pen much, either, but I do admire the way she thinks."

"Have you forgiven her for nearly killing you, then?" I say.

"I admire it, really. She's not the sort to hide bodies or make pleasantries; with her one always knows where one stands. If I'm to choose anyone for my council, it's a girl who has no regard for hierarchy." He gives me a sharp look. "But I order you never to tell her that."

"Oh, but of course, Your Majesty."

He turns his back to the window and squints at me. "What do you know of her family? Pen's."

My knees go weak, and I disguise it by leaning beside him against the window ledge. "She's an only child. Her mother is reclusive. Her father works longer hours than most—but you know that already. It's on the record."

"You must know more than that," he presses. "The two of you are as close to each other as I am to my sister. I can tell. It's this nearly psychic connection."

"Like a double birth," I say, echoing something Pen has used to describe us before.

"So you surely must know more than that."

I look at him. "Would you give Celeste's secrets up so easily?"

His smile is fond and sad. "You'd have to cut them from my veins."

"So then you understand."

"Can't blame a king for trying."

"Pen is an only child," I say again. "Her parents didn't reenter the queue. That's about all there is to tell."

"I've been going through my father's records these last few days. You know there's a sheet written about everyone in the city. Medical records, mostly. Allergies. Behavioral mishaps. Pen's mother has quite a few notes."

Yes, I'd imagine she does.

"Her father's sheet, however . . ." He trails off. I think he's waiting to see if I'll interject. When I don't, he says, "There are certain marks in public records to denote repeat offenses and vices—tonic addiction, disturbing the peace, people who have been to the attraction camps, jumpers, what have you. But Pen's father's record is utterly flawless, excepting a black dot by his name."

A black dot. That's all there is to hold him accountable for what he's done. Pen was strong enough to survive it, but there is far more than a dot of ink marking her.

"I don't know what it means," the new king says. "But my father had a way of forgiving crimes if they were committed by someone he deemed useful. And Nolan Atmus is indeed useful, but in a way that I'd like to keep at arm's length. What is your thought on that?"

I take a deep breath. "My thought is that, if you don't refer to her as Margaret, and you don't bring up the black dot, Pen will be happy to help you."

"Splendid!" His sudden cheer is a relief. "Let's go pay her a visit, then."

Pen is weak but entirely lucid when the new king and I enter her hospital room. She gives him a wry smile. "To whatever do I owe the honor, Your Majesty?"

He ignores the jab, and she brightens considerably when she sees the drawing paper he's brought her. "We're to design a flight path between Internment and Havalais, and calculate the impact it will have on our city's new tendency to sink."

She reaches for the paper greedily. "I've already done all the measurements."

As she explains the impact the jet has on Internment's altitude, the new king says nothing of his plans. He asks questions that Pen is all too happy to answer. On a separate sheet, she draws the sunstone itself, explaining how the flecks within the soil are compressed and refined in a way not dissimilar from coal. And when he's had enough, he rolls her drawings up neatly and tucks them under his arm.

"Where are you going?" Pen says as he heads for the door.

"To mull and brood," he says, quite decisively. "It takes a great deal of that to run a kingdom."

Hours later, King Azure summons me outside of the tower. The sun has just set, and he carries a lantern but doesn't light it. Wherever we're going, he doesn't want us to be seen even by the patrolmen meant to protect him.

There's a chill in the air, but it's a relief in contrast to the stuffiness of the clock tower. I don't know how the royal family can stand to live so high up in all that stale air, especially during the long season, when the air is like bath steam.

Once he has led me away from the patrolmen, he lights the lantern. We walk in silence for what feels like an hour before he says, "When we were children, my sister and I would compete for our father's attention. But we did so knowing that I would be the one to inherit the kingdom, and so when Papa confided in me alone, I reveled in it. I did enjoy torturing my sister with knowledge she couldn't have."

"Now you sound like my brother," I say, and brace myself against the pain that fills my chest with those words. I do miss him and Alice quite much.

"One day," he goes on, "Papa led me through the woods. Celeste wasn't invited. At first I was rather smug about it. Important. But the farther on we went, the more I began to worry. I had never been so deep into the woods before, and this sort of . . . dread filled my stomach."

I also never thought the woods ran this deep. It's as though we've stepped into a parallel world that's twice as large as our floating city. He looks at me as though to determine whether I'm afraid. But I've spent years trying to navigate the darkness of my brother's mind. A few trees and a starlit sky are of no concern to me.

"What's out here?" I ask.

"Something my father didn't want the city to see." He raises the lantern, opens the door, and blows out the flame.

It takes a moment for my eyes to adjust to the darkness, and then I see slivers of light up ahead, peeking out from what appear to be buildings clustered together behind a fence.

And I understand.

"These are the attraction camps," I say.

"Yes," King Azure says. "It's the first thing I mean to destroy, as king. Normally there would be more patrolmen standing guard, but they're all preoccupied now, as you can imagine. We can get closer, but we must be quiet. I don't want anyone to know that you've seen this."

He is as silent as a hunter, the way he moves, and I do my best to mimic this.

He crouches before the fence. "Here," he whispers. "You can see into that window there."

I kneel beside him, gathering the skirts of my borrowed dress. I follow his gaze and I see a woman with cloth wrapped around her mouth, spooning liquid to a body lying on a bed. It's hard to believe the body is alive, but I think I see it breathe.

"I've put a stop to the surgeries," he says.

"Surgeries?" When I crane my neck, I'm just able to see the body on the bed. It looks like a child whose head has been shaved. My heart leaps up into my throat. "They do something to their brains," I breathe.

The king's silence is his answer. I'm glad that he can't take me farther than this. I do not want to see what exists in those other buildings without any windows at all.

"It's gone on for more than a century," King Azure says. "As I understand, it began as an experiment to correct the boys who were attracted to boys, the girls who were attracted to girls, and the ones who seemed to be attracted to both or neither."

"Has it ever worked?" I ask, horrified.

"The records say yes, but I think not," he says. "If I had to endure what goes on in that place, I'd be more inclined to lie and say I was healed, wouldn't you?"

I've begun to feel dizzy. I press my lips tightly together and try not to be sick.

"My father took a special interest in this place, even as a boy, before he was king. And its purpose has expanded since then to include criminals and traitors—anyone he means to change. When they recover, they're never quite the same. They have seizures, or memory loss, or they can scarcely walk. In some cases they become entirely dependent on their betrothed to take care of them."

I think of the woman who used to live in my apartment building. Every day she would follow her betrothed to the doorway and then stand there to watch him go. I wonder if she was once here.

"It's awful," I say.

"I mean to have this entire facility demolished," he says. "Let it become a field for livestock. Let it reek of manure. That would suit me just fine."

In the dim light of faraway buildings, I see the fear in his bright eyes. And I know that being a prince would not have spared him this fate, if only his father had known the truth about him.

"Your Majesty," I say, "I'm so sorry."

"Don't be." He blinks and comes back to himself. "I've brought you here to show you that you've done me a favor. This place could never be destroyed while my father was alive. You did what I wish I could have done a long time ago."

I'm stunned that he would see my killing his father as a favor, even if I'm starting to agree. We begin walking, and I look over my shoulder at that horrible shadow of a tiny city. I know what he was trying to tell me. After the king attempted to murder his own grandchild to save the royal reputation, I have no doubt.

I fear speaking, but I know that I have to.

"Was my father in there?"

He looks at me, the candlelight casting long shadows

on his face. "I can't say for certain. After you left for the ground, many patrolmen were killed for their insubordination. Others professed their loyalty. And others, yes, did end up in the attraction camps. The primary purpose is to change—or attempt to change—one's sexual attraction. But that's really only the start of it. My father believed any facets of the mind could be changed with surgery."

I veer around and start pacing toward the camp. King Azure grabs my arm. "Morgan, don't."

I try to break free, but his grip only tightens.

"Let me go!"

"Would you lower your voice?" he says through gritted teeth. "I didn't show you this place so that you could go charging in there causing a scene. I may be in charge of the kingdom now, but I'm still determining which members of my father's council can be trusted, and I can't have you putting yourself at risk."

"He's my father," I bite back. "He's one of the few people I have left. You would go back if you thought Celeste were in there!"

"Yes," he says. "Yes, I would burn the bloody place to the ground if I had to. But Celeste isn't in there, and neither is your father. I checked."

I stop struggling, and cautiously he lets go of my arm, watching and ready to apprehend me if I run again. But I don't. My legs feel rubbery and numb. "You checked? What does that mean?"

"After my father's death, while you were recovering, there was much for me to do. It isn't as easy as just becoming king, you know. I had to assess the damage, so to speak. That included going through the attraction camps and learning the status of each patient—"

"Victim, you mean."

"If you'd rather. And I put a stop to the surgeries and instructed the nurses to return the victims to health. I saw every face in every bed, and there were no grown men left at all."

My breath hitches. "Left?"

He hesitates. "There's an incinerator for the patients who don't make it."

"The ones your father didn't want to make it," I say. I'm struggling to draw each breath, and I can't bear the look of pity in the king's eyes. I lost my parents once already, and I did not think that sharp pain of the initial realization could repeat itself, but now I see that it can. There is no limit to how much pain can be felt in a life.

Lex is the only person in either world who could understand. I wish that he were here. I would even take his cynicism, his "That's the way it is, Little Sister. What did you expect?" if he had no comfort to offer.

But I can't have even that much. All that's left of my family is gone from this floating city. There is no one waiting for me at our apartment. It's only me.

21

Celeste is not the fool her brother makes her out
to be. She has heard the full report of everything that happened the night her father was slain. She has heard that a
maddened patrolman killed her father, and that I was the
one to fight the patrolman off.

I can tell, however, that she doesn't believe a word of
it. We don't speak in the days before her brother's coronation, and the truth lingers in the air between us, something
between what she has heard and what she fears.

Hours before her brother is to become king, I find her
sitting on the top step before my chamber door, dragging
her fingertip across her daughter's face.

"What do they know?"

I stop ascending the stairs and hold fast to the banister.
She's just close enough that she could extend her foot and
kick me to my death to avenge her father if she wanted.

When I don't answer, she raises her head. It's the first time she's truly looked at me since the ordeal that night, and I'm surprised at the lack of malice in her eyes. She looks only curious.

"What does who know?" I ask.

"The kingdom," she says. "Have they heard about my daughter?"

Strange, I think, that a child with such an important role to play remains nameless.

"There have been rumors about a child," I say. "The night we ran for the jet, some people heard her crying. But they suspect she's the child of a mistress your brother has been keeping. Or that he rescued a fugitive from the ground and the child is hers. It's hard to tell what they think—it changes by the hour."

Her sharp laugh hits the walls of the stairwell like a dozen slaps. "That figures he'd get the credit, even for this. Do you know my brother has been in conference with Nim all morning? 'One king to another' he says. I'm not even invited. Fancy that."

"It's safer for you if the citizens believe the rumor," I say. I mean to console her, and it's also the truth. "There's too much danger if the kingdom finds out you've had a child outside of the queue. It's forbidden."

She shakes her head. "Dead kings dictated our history books, and male appointees transcribed them, Morgan. I wonder how many daughters and sisters and mothers wrote the stories that never made it onto the page."

I know just what she's thinking: She wants to announce

her handiwork to her kingdom. She wants to give them their new child of two worlds, and she believes they'll love it the way she believed her father would love it. I know, also, that she can't be talked out of her ideas once she's had them. But still I'm going to try.

Cautiously, I approach and sit beside her. "Celeste." My voice is soft. "I think what you've done is incredibly brave. I do. And, with time, the two kingdoms will see it as well. Your brother will do away with the queue, and when he opens up a flight path to the ground, everyone will have more freedom than they can fathom. They'll thank you for that."

She looks at me.

"But," I go on, "right now, all they will see is that you have something they can't have. You were allowed a right that would be taken from them. They'll hate you for it."

"Some will," she says. "But I don't care about that. It isn't my mission in life to be liked. It's my mission to do what's right for Internment and Havalais. I'm here to change things. It's why I was born; I've always known that, even before I knew what it meant."

"And you *will*," I assure her.

"Just not today, is that it?"

"Nothing grand can be accomplished in a single day," I say.

"Oh, I beg to differ." She stands, and for all her fire, she must move slowly and cringing all the while. She shouldn't be out of bed at all, if she were to take her doctor's advice.

Her brother told me that it was a torturous labor. After hours of watching his daughter struggle, the king ordered the doctor to render her unconscious and to cut the child from her stomach. He was certain her screams could be heard throughout the kingdom and he wanted it over with. Prince Azure could only listen outside the locked door as his sister fell silent.

That was the most he would speak of it. Celeste said nothing of it at all. She is not the sort of person to acknowledge something so unhelpful as pain.

"We aren't different, you and I," Celeste says. "We don't treat rules as though they're walls. I suppose I was just born surrounded by bigger barriers to climb."

"Sometimes it's wise to pretend to have no interest in climbing," I say.

In her sad smile I can't tell if my words have reached her. I hope that they have.

The coronation ceremony is to take place in the evening. The new king and Nimble have been in conference for days, with Celeste growing all the more anxious.

At last, with three hours before the ceremony, the door to the king's study opens and we're invited inside.

It's a bizarre council for a king. His advisers consist of Pen, Celeste, and myself. He's still determining whether Basil is trustworthy. The table could easily seat a dozen heads. Past kings might have chosen as few as three advisers, though all of them would have been men, and all of them much older and better versed in the old ways than we are.

But this king does not care for the old ways, and we are the only ones on this floating city whom he can truly trust.

"So kind of you to finally invite us in, Brother," Celeste says, breezing past him and taking the seat beside Nimble, who looks at her with concern. Though there's color in her cheeks and she looks well, something has changed. She's aged years in just a few days.

Her hair falls straight before her rigid shoulders, with no braided crown. She's wearing a loose button-up dress that hides her figure, with a lace collar that just brushes her clenched jaw. She looks a decade older than the mischievous princess who stowed away on the metal bird. Nonetheless she still looks the part of the princess Internment loves — pretty and benign.

"Celeste," the new king says, "I've invited you here so that we might get through this bloody ceremony as a team. But for that to work, I need you to trust me without having a tantrum about hierarchy."

"Tantrum?" She looks at him innocently. "Of course not, Your Majesty. I'm only the spare. Here to serve."

He rubs his temples and sighs. To the group of us he says, "None of us has ever been to a coronation ceremony, but throughout history they've been transcribed, and I can tell you from the pages I've just slogged through that they are long and insufferable. This won't be one of those."

"Won't it have to be?" Pen says. "You're declaring so many changes to our law."

"It hasn't been all fun and games behind this locked door," he says. "I've written several new laws and arranged for copies to be delivered to every home. I believe it's better this way. More organized."

The new king sits uneasily at the head of the table, still wearing one of his white ruffled shirts. He looks nothing at all like a king, and I worry over whether he'll be able to command this city.

"The feature of my coronation speech will be with regards to the ground," he says. "Pen has done the math, and it's her prediction that it will take roughly five years for Internment to resurface to its coordinates before the jet began making passage. Knowing that, Nimble—being the king of Havalais now—will head a project to build aircrafts that will travel between the two kingdoms. If all goes well, there will be a larger jet that will carry citizens between the two kingdoms every five years."

Celeste looks between her brother and Nim. "Five years?" she says. "Where will I be during that time?"

Here the new king pauses. No emotion registers on his face, but I can see that he's holding his breath and there's a slight twitching in his thumb. "You and your child will be on the ground," he says. "Someone with royal blood from Internment must be there to oversee the project and to serve as a representative of our kingdom. There's no one better suited than you."

Celeste stares, with wide, dazed eyes, at nothing in particular. She wanted an important role, but I doubt this was what she had in mind.

"Five years." Her voice is a whisper. She looks at King Azure. "When will we leave?"

"Tomorrow morning."

"But what about Mother?"

He can't give her an answer she'll want to hear. No one speaks, and the silence rises up around us like waves. When I can bear it no longer, I say, "King Ingram had a radio that he used to communicate with your father, didn't he?"

"Yes," the new king says, and clears his throat. "Pen has been tinkering with that."

"It's a bit archaic, but functional," Pen offers. "It operates on radio waves, and as long as there's something to pick up the frequency, it will work." She glances at me for an instant and then away. "I've volunteered to return to Havalais and prepare weekly reports, and technology will be one of the things I observe."

A stone-solid weight sinks in my stomach. And suddenly five years feels like a lifetime.

The new king must pick up on my worry, because he leans toward me and says, "Morgan, I'd very much prefer if you stayed here. You know more than I do about the day-to-day life in this city. You've grown up in the public, unlike my sister and me. Your family had a jumper and you've been subjected to specialists. You know more than anyone the importance of changing the way of things. And I dare to say I trust you."

I can't draw a full breath. I hide my hands under the table to conceal their trembling. Though I don't look at her, I can feel Pen's eyes watching me.

"I'd have to think about it, Your Majesty," I say.

"Yes, do," he says.

He goes on talking about the changes he means to make in the city, but I can't retain a word of it. Five years away from my brother and Alice. Five years in this city, where my mother is dead and my father is nowhere to be found. Basil would prefer to stay—I know that. He would be with his family again.

But what do I want?

There's a chill under my skin that won't warm. After the meeting has ended, I am the first through the door. I stumble dazedly down the stairwell and out to the garden, where the poppies pool like blood against the cobbles.

If I focus on the center of all the flowers, I stop seeing the edges of the petals, and it becomes a red ocean. The people of Internment can never know the beauty and the terror of all that water below us, filled with fish and animals that could swallow us whole. And the mermaids, and the lights glittering from the harbor. All my life I wondered what lay below this city, and the truth is so much bigger and more fantastic than I could have imagined.

In five years I could see so much more of it. Without Jack Piper to dictate my every move and exploit me for his gain, I could even leave Havalais. I wouldn't have to report back to any king.

I don't know how long I sit there, mystified by all the possibilities, before Basil sits beside me.

I lean against him, and he wraps his arm around my shoulders. It's one thing to know I love him, but quite another to be reminded in this way of how easily my body fits against his, like coming home.

At last, he says, "Pen told me about your meeting with the king."

I breathe out the weight that's been crushing my chest. "So you know about his offer, then." I look from the poppies to the sky, with its thin wisps of clouds. The sky is always blue here, always calm, even when it's storming below us. "I don't think I can do it, Basil. I don't think I can stay here for five years. Not if I have the chance to leave."

"Then you shouldn't." He says it with such ease, as though he's always known it would come to this. "It's five years, not an eternity. You could always come back if you wanted."

His body is warm and familiar against mine, and I know that for all the wonders the ground holds, there is nothing like this feeling that I belong. I will always want to come back to him.

Though I dread the answer, I ask, "What will you do if I go?"

He's quiet for a long while, and then he says, "I love you for your adventurous spirit, Morgan, as much as I have always feared it. All my life, I've thought that a day would come when you'd hitch a ride on the wind and soar off into the sky."

I sit up and turn to face him. "That isn't what I'm doing. You know that, don't you?"

He smiles. "Yes, I know. But if this opportunity had arisen when we were children, I would have tried to make you stay. I would have thought that it was up to me to protect you. The idea of letting go would have terrified me."

"Basil . . ."

"But I'd rather watch you sail off into the sky than try to keep you here for my sake."

"You think I should go, then."

"You didn't need me to tell you that."

I stare down at my betrothal band, perhaps never to be filled with his blood now that the new king will be doing away with assigned betrothals. These little glass rings have seen thousands upon thousands of marriages. But none has ever been worn by a girl who went off to explore the world alone.

It's only five years, I remind myself. It isn't forever.

22

I don't have a chance to give the king an
answer before the coronation ceremony.

I borrow one of Celeste's dresses—a soft yellow that
reminds me of falling leaves—and follow everyone down
the stairs. Along the way, Pen takes my hand and holds
tight. She doesn't know yet what my decision will be. I
wonder if Thomas will follow her to the ground, but I
know that it won't change her mind one way or the other.
She's going, with or without him. With or without me.

We've both grown so much in less than a year's time.
We're less afraid to face life on our own. I know that she
won't try to convince me one way or the other, nor will I
for her. We will not always be in the same city. We will float
off in opposite directions to explore the worlds, and find
each other again and again through the years, reveling in
the changes we've made while we were apart.

King Azure stands upon a makeshift stage that is centuries old. Its boards creak with his steps. Internment can never compare to the grandeur of the ground. This is no glittering palace the size of a city. But up here, we don't lose ourselves in the illusion of fineries. This king does not mean to dazzle, merely to reign.

Hundreds of people have come to witness the dawning of a new king. It happens only once in a lifetime, and I suspect the entire city would be here if only it were possible to fit them all in front of the clock tower.

A patrolman is managing the camera that will broadcast the event. King Azure is surrounded by a wall of patrolmen as he begins his coronation speech. As always, Celeste stands in her usual place beside him. But unlike in the other broadcasts, the pair of them don't look bored. There is something fierce in their eyes.

When he speaks, he doesn't get deep into the politics. He focuses mainly on the ground, and that his sister will oversee the development of new aircrafts. In five years, he promises aircrafts large enough to transport as many as fifty passengers at a time. And in the future, perhaps a hundred. Perhaps more. The future is all about expansion.

Celeste is regal and as still as a statue, and I wonder if the prospect of returning to Havalais has left her in a daze. All day I've had a horrible feeling that she will announce the birth of her child or something equally damning. But she doesn't, and once the ceremony is through, I'm relieved. I think she is too. She flees from the stage the moment the speech is over. Her brother turns to her for reassurance, and he's met with only the crowd closing in to speak to him.

Someone asks him about the princess's health. She was rumored to be at death's door just a few days ago, after all.

"The king talks to his citizens?" Nim says.

"Of course," I say. "But then, he doesn't have a castle to retreat to. Not like you will once you return."

"Oh, that old thing," Nim says. "Celeste thinks I ought to use it for something public. A shelter of sorts. I think she's onto something." He cranes his neck and searches the crowd. "Where is she?"

"Hiding away somewhere, I'm sure." I nudge him. "You should go inside and look for her."

Once he's gone, I slip through the crowd and begin making my way to the woods. I don't want King Azure to find me. Not yet. Not until I'm ready to answer his proposal.

Just when I've broken free of the ceremony, someone grabs my arm and reels me back. I expect Pen, here to scold me about leaving her to fend for herself in that commotion, but instead I find myself staring into the face of a boy I don't recognize.

He's almost too flawless to be real. A well-colored drawing in one of Birdie's fashion magazines, not a blond hair on his head out of place. "Don't run off so soon," he says, his voice as gentle as it is menacing. "I have so wanted to meet the girl who's been to the ground and back. Morgan, isn't it? I'm Virgil."

In our history book, Virgil was the name of a scribe who fell in love with an uncorrupted who became a star in the sky after she died. Her name was Celeste.

I pull my arm free of his grip. It's all so very on-the-nose. So this is the boy the princess was fated to marry, the one who was conceived just to be her match.

The historical Virgil did not end up with the historical Celeste, and I wonder if this boy has realized yet that history will repeat itself.

"Yes," I say. "Is there something I can help you with?"

His lip quirks into a lopsided smile that might be charming if I didn't know how hated he is by Celeste and her brother. "Eager to please," he says. "I like that."

Eager to be rid of him is all.

"I was hoping you could tell me where my betrothed has run off to. She was gone the moment her brother finally stopped droning on."

"If you'd paid any attention to his droning, you'd know that she's not your betrothed any longer."

He sighs as though this is all a trivial inconvenience. "It will be amusing to watch this child king test the waters. But that's one decree that won't stick, I'm certain. In any case, have you seen her?"

"I haven't, no," I say.

"I've been by several times since her return from the ground," he says. "I was turned away at every instance and led to believe she was at death's door. Imagine my relief to see her alive and well. A miraculous recovery brought on by the excitement of her brother's new role, I suppose."

"It seems that way," I say. With his cool stare he has made me second-guess my decision to go into the woods alone. I look past him, into the milling crowd that seems to be moving, as endlessly as the ocean's waves, in King Azure's direction.

"Would you be so kind as to give her this?" He has extracted a folded note from his breast pocket. "When you see her again."

"All right," I say, and am relieved that this will be the end of it. Even as he turns back into the crowd, he is looking for her, though surely he knows that this will prove futile. She's long gone by now, and half a dozen patrolmen are guarding the only open entrance to the clock tower.

I look at the paper resting in my palm. It has been folded into a perfect square, tied with a length of string. If it's a profession of love, I'm sure that it's insincere.

"Who was that?" Basil has moved to my side.

"Celeste's betrothed."

His eyes widen. "Really. So that's him."

"I wondered why she ran off so quickly after the speech. Now I know."

Basil points to a girl talking to King Azure. From this distance I can just see her light hair pinned atop her head. "That's his betrothed."

"Really?" I stand up on tiptoes to try to have a better look. "How do you know?"

"He introduced her to me. They seem to have a cordial relationship, at least."

I wonder if she knows the full truth about him and his desires. From where I stand, they seem to be laughing as they talk.

"I was just about to run off and hide," I say. "Care to join me?"

He grins. "Always."

We hold hands as we walk. Neither of us planned it; it just seems to happen. We fit together.

"I've made a decision," I say, and though he says nothing, I can feel his body tensing. "Once the ceremony is over, I'll tell the king that he's presented me with a flattering offer, but I must decline." I lean forward so I can see Basil's face. He looks at me. "I'm going to the ground," I tell him. "It's not forever. Only until the next flight to Internment, and then I'll come back. I'll have to. It will always call to me."

He forces a smile. "Good," he says. "I wouldn't have believed you if you'd told me you wanted to stay."

"Basil . . ." I nearly lose my nerve. My heart is beating fast and there's pain tangled up in the fear and excitement. "When we first left Internment, you chose to come with me. You chose to leave your family, and I—I was happy that you did, but it's not a one-way venture anymore. It's not forever. You don't have to choose and neither do I."

He nods. "I was thinking the same." He stops our walking, and he turns to face me. "I need to be with my family now. They're scared, and Leland is so young—I want to be there for him as he grows up. They almost lost me once, I don't want to leave them again."

"Five years isn't forever," I remind him. "And I'll radio in when Pen reports back to the king." I squeeze his hand. "I'll tell you everything."

"I'll be there every broadcast," he says.

"Remind me—remind me of what Internment is like, every time we talk," I say. "While I was on the ground, I think I began to forget bits and pieces of it."

He stares at me a long while, and we say nothing. But when he brushes his hand across my cheek, I fall against him and squeeze my eyes shut to ward off the tears.

"I've loved you all my life," I say.

His arms circle around me. "I've loved you, too."

Later, in the starry silence, Basil and I spend our last night together. We don't guess at what will become of us in five years. We don't imagine the things we'll see or the ways we'll change. We say nothing, absolutely nothing, and in the darkness our bodies find each other, his asking permission, mine drawing him in.

It's painful, and peaceful, and in its own way, freeing. We draw each other as close as we can. And then we let each other go.

23

There's a knock at our bedroom door before the sun has fully risen in its sky. "Morgan?" Pen's voice. She doesn't open the door. "The king wants us downstairs in ten minutes. Are you awake?"

"Yes," I say. "I'll be there."

Basil and I get dressed. I wear another of Celeste's borrowed dresses—white with an eyelet skirt and a red ribbon laced up the bodice—and I realize that it's the only piece of clothing from Internment I'll bring with me to the ground, and it isn't even mine.

The only other thing I carry is my ring, which gleams dully in the early light. Basil and I made no promises to wear them. I don't know if he'll still be wearing his when I return in five years, and I don't know if I'll still be wearing mine. But for now, it comforts me.

We descend the stairs, and King Azure is waiting for us

in the lobby, Celeste at his side, holding her infant in the crook of her arm and rubbing her reddened eyes as though she's been crying all night. After the ceremony, she went into her mother's bedroom and closed the door. She wanted to spend her last hours in this city by her mother's side. After everything, it was the only time they would have left.

Nimble, Pen, and Thomas are talking to one another in low voices nearby. So Thomas has decided to follow Pen. That doesn't surprise me. He wouldn't know how to breathe without her, and I suppose that's a good thing, because she needs him every bit as much, only she's too proud to tell him so. Telling him she was going to the ground was as close as she'd get to asking him to follow.

"Did I tell you?" Celeste says to me when I approach. "I've thought of a name for my daughter. At first I thought 'Riles,' for Nim's brother, but 'Riley' is much more fitting for a girl, don't you think?" She runs her finger against the infant's cheek fondly. "It's a strong name. The name of a girl who won't take an injustice quietly. One who will incite a riot if she needs to."

"I've the feeling she would be willing to do that no matter what her name is," I say. "She's your daughter after all."

Celeste laughs, and it's the first time I've seen her smile in days. "Yes," she says.

There are a dozen patrolmen surrounding us when we make our way to the jet. It will be a crowded flight, as many of the men from the ground will also be returning with us.

"I apologize that it won't be much of a grand send-off,"

King Azure says. "I didn't want there to be a crowd. It's unsafe for you."

"A crowd is the last thing any of us wants," Celeste says. Nim is holding their daughter now, and he looks considerably more rested. He was sent to his chambers early, with a pill to help him sleep. It's his job to fly us home, and King Azure insisted that he not be disturbed until morning.

The jet is waiting for us on the other side of the tracks, and Basil remains by my side until we've reached the metal staircase that leads inside.

This is it. This is where I leave him.

When we first left Internment, and the metal bird began sinking toward the sky, Pen broke into a sudden panic; she would have done anything to remain on Internment, even knowing that to leave the bird was to die.

I understand that panic now. For the first time, I truly understand it. I'm terrified to leave, overtaken by the finality of my decision. In five years, this city will have changed without me. Basil will be older. I'll be older. We'll both have learned who we are without each other.

If I stayed here, I could marry him tomorrow. In five years, without the queue we could even have a child.

I could stay. I could.

But I would never forgive myself. The things I love about Internment would turn into the things I'd resent for holding me back. And so I say, "Good-bye." Not only to Basil, but to all I'm leaving behind.

He kisses me once, briefly. "Good-bye."

The warmth of his lips, I'm certain, will stay with me

the entire way down, just like the dull pain deep within my hips that reminds me of the night before.

Everyone else has said their good-byes and boarded the jet. I'm the last to go.

"Stop!" a voice cries out, just as Pen and Celeste are guiding me into the jet's entrance. For one bereft, dazed instant I think that it's Basil saying that he'll come with me. But no, the voice does not belong to him.

Celeste's eyes narrow and she pushes past me. "What do you want, Virgil?"

Her ex-betrothed is scrambling over the train tracks and running toward us. He doesn't make it far. The patrolmen step into action, but it's King Azure who grabs him and pins his arms behind his back. Virgil struggles. "I knew you would try to sneak off without me. I demand to go with you!"

Celeste rubs her palms over her eyes, exasperated. "If you want to see the ground, you'll have your opportunity in five years. On your own."

"You can't go without me," he calls out. "We're meant to be together. I was born to be your other."

"What's done is done. We're nothing to each other now. I suggest you go on and have your own future. I'm off to start mine."

"There's someone else, isn't there?" he snaps. "I knew that must be it. You've been maddened by lust!"

Celeste stands tall. She is no longer a child who needs to run to the poppies to be free of him. "There's always been someone else," she says. "Me."

She pulls the door shut with a slam, and the latches fall into place.

The engines burst to life, and I rush to the tiny oval window to catch one last glimpse of Internment before it's gone. In seconds we're moving, and Basil is too far away for me to see his face. He stands still to watch me go, even with the dirt and the wind in his hair.

And then we've broken through the wind barrier, and when the clouds have cleared, I can no longer see him.

Pen and Celeste put their arms around me, and together we watch our city become a shadow in the sky, and then nothing at all.

"Once we land, where will you go?" Pen asks me.

"Everywhere," I say.

broken
crowns

also by
Lauren
DeStefano

The Internment Chronicles
perfect ruin
burning kingdoms

The Internment Chronicles e-novellas
no intention of dying
the heir apparent

The Chemical Garden Trilogy
wither
fever
sever